HAPPY
HALLOWEEN
THIS BOOK
BELONGS TO

GET READY TO LAUGH YOUR SOCKS OFF WITH THIS HILARIOUS COLLECTION OF HALLOWEEN JOKES!

THIS BOOK IS PACKED WITH SPOOKY PUNS, BONE-CHILLING ONE-LINERS, AND GHOULISH GAGS THAT ARE SURE TO MAKE YOU HOWL WITH LAUGHTER. WHETHER YOU'RE LOOKING FOR JOKES TO TELL AT A HALLOWEEN PARTY, OR JUST WANT TO ADD SOME SPOOKY FUN TO YOUR DAY, THIS BOOK HAS SOMETHING FOR YOU.

"TRICK OR TREAT: WOULD YOU RATHER?"

GET READY FOR A SPOOKY SEASON OF LAUGHTER WITH "TRICK OR TREAT: WOULD YOU RATHER?" THIS SPINE-CHILLING COLLECTION OF "WOULD YOU RATHER" QUESTIONS WILL HAVE YOU HOWLING WITH LAUGHTER.

FROM GHOULISH GOBLINS TO TERRIFYING TRICK-OR-TREATERS, EACH QUESTION WILL PUT YOU IN A HALLOWEEN DILEMMA. WILL YOU CHOOSE TO SPEND ETERNITY WITH A VAMPIRE OR A WEREWOLF?
WOULD YOU RATHER BE CHASED BY A ZOMBIE OR A GHOST?

My life is like a roll of toilet paper - long and useful, but it always seems to be circling the drain.

My friend said I don't know jack shit. I said "Au contraire, I know John Shit, Jim Shit, and the whole Shit family."

Life's like a sewer... what you get out of it depends on what you put into it.

Shit has no solution... but ghost poop is a supernatural suspension.

Shit happens, but so does toilet paper.

My therapist told me to embrace my mistakes.
So I gave myself a hug.

Life's like a septic tank:
the big chunks always rise to the top.
I'm on a seafood diet. I see food, and then I eat it.
Ghost poop is like my love life - I'm pretty sure it exists, but I can never seem to find any evidence.

The best Halloween costume?
Ghost poop. You don't have to wear anything and still scare the crap out of people.
Shit is like knowledge - the more you spread it, the worse it smells.
Shit has no solution... but it sure has a lot of dissolution.

I'm not saying I'm the shit, but I could definitely fertilize a field.
I tried to record the sound of ghost poop.
All I got was 10 hours of toilet bowl ambiance.
I wanted to be a proctologist, but I couldn't stand all the assholes.

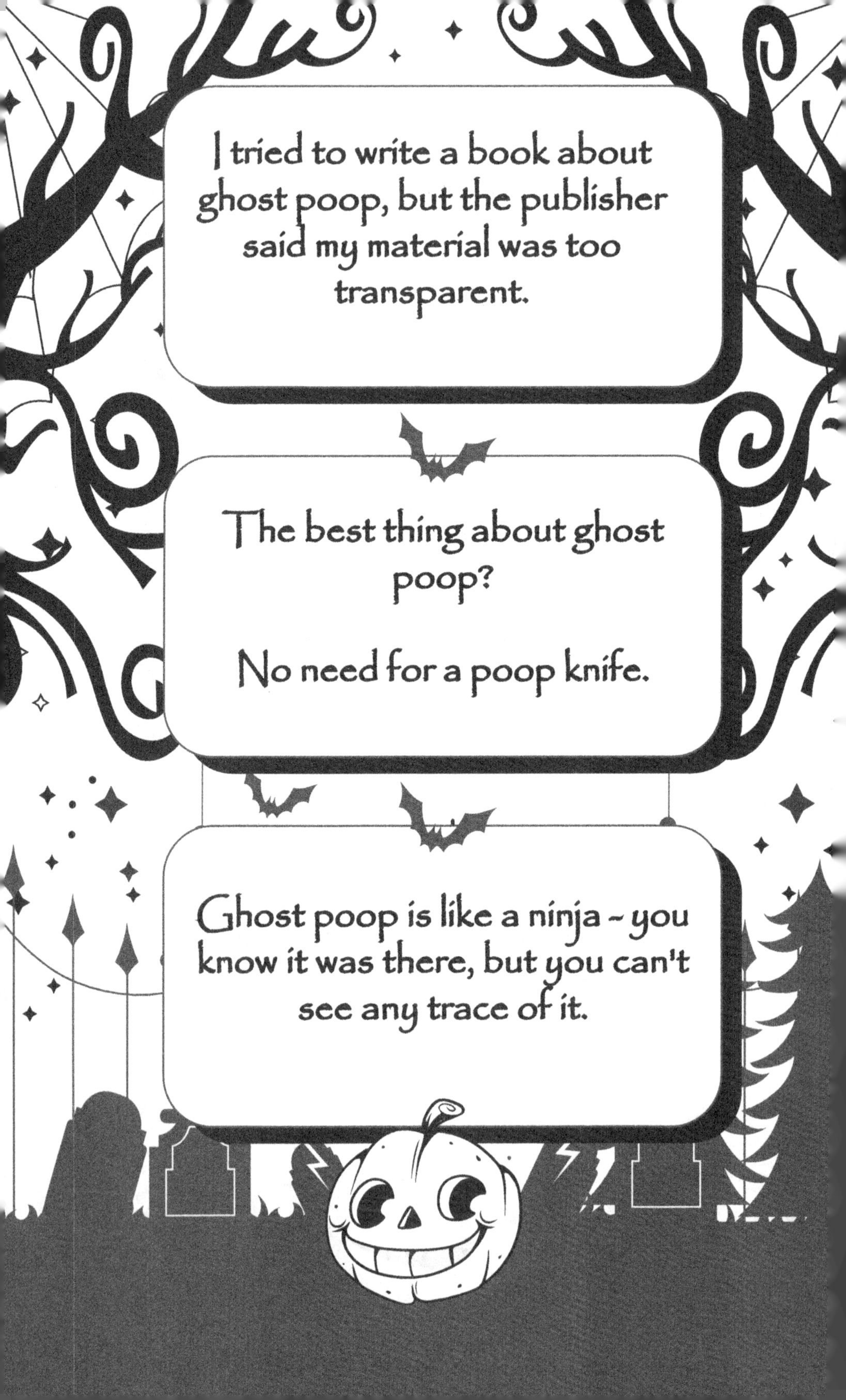
I tried to write a book about ghost poop, but the publisher said my material was too transparent.
The best thing about ghost poop?
No need for a poop knife.
Ghost poop is like a ninja - you know it was there, but you can't see any trace of it.

How do ghosts poop?

They let out a boo-boo!

How do phantoms freshen up after using the bathroom?

They use BOO-pourri!

I always ask how ghost poop... but the answer just passes right through me.

I always wonder how ghost poop... I guess it's just another unsolved mystery of the supernatural movements.
I always wonder how ghost poop... I guess it's just another unsolved mystery of the supernatural movements.
when you feel like you've done your business, but the toilet paper comes up clean. It's the paranormal activity of the porcelain throne!

I asked a psychic about my ghost poop. She said she sensed a movement in my future.
I asked a medium about ghost poop. She said she couldn't comment because it was too personal a matter.
Ghost poop is the ultimate diet food - all the feeling of fullness with none of the calories.

What do you call a fake noodle?

An impasta!

I tried to use ghost poop as fertilizer. My plants are now invisible, but they smell fantastic!

I tried to patent ghost poop, but the patent office said my claim lacked substance.

What do you call a constipated ghost?

A stubborn sheet!

What do witches use to unclog their toilets?

Hex-Drano!

What do vampires use to fix leaky faucets?

Bat-htub caulk!

What do vampires use instead of toilet paper?
Bat wings!
What do you call a ghost who's always getting into trouble?
A boo-hoo-ligan!
What do you call a ghost's favorite plunger?
A boo-unger!

What's it like to be kissed by a vampire?

It's a pain in the neck.

What's the difference between a ghost and a bad joke?

A bad joke is just plain bad, but a ghost is haunting!

Why are ghosts bad at hide-and-seek?

Because you can see right through them!

Where do baby ghosts go during the day?

Dayscare centers!

What's the most important subject in vampire school?

Blood-ology!

What's the problem with twin witches?

You never know which one you're talking to!

Would you rather:
Have to organize a monster prom where everyone has conflicting dietary requirements OR plan a haunted house where the ghosts are on strike?

Would you rather:
Be cursed to always walk as if you're tip-toeing through a haunted house OR have to dramatically gasp every time you enter a room?

Would you rather:
Have to wear a mask that changes your personality every hour OR shoes that force you to dance to spooky music whenever you hear it?

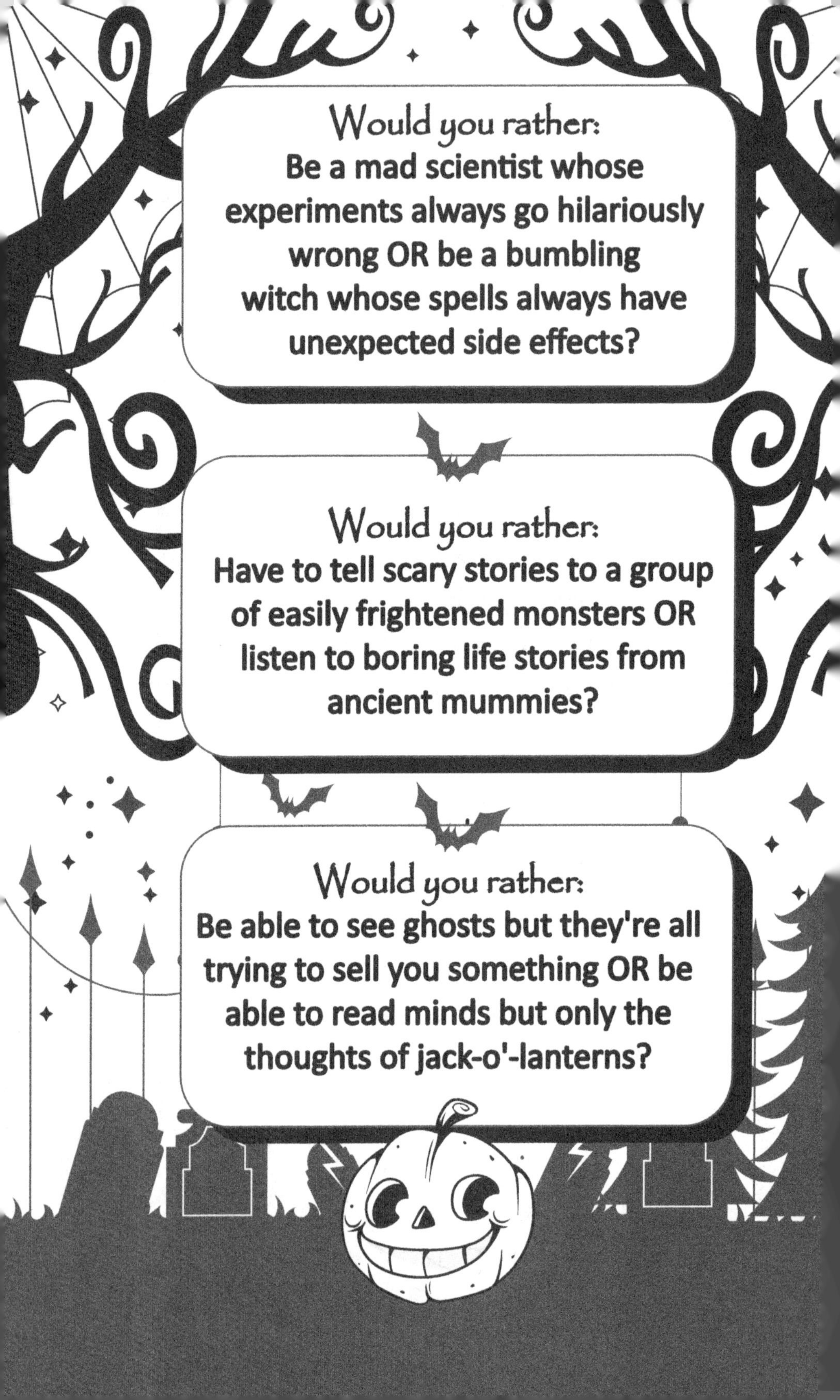
Would you rather:
Be a mad scientist whose experiments always go hilariously wrong OR be a bumbling witch whose spells always have unexpected side effects?
Would you rather:
Have to tell scary stories to a group of easily frightened monsters OR listen to boring life stories from ancient mummies?
Would you rather:
Be able to see ghosts but they're all trying to sell you something OR be able to read minds but only the thoughts of jack-o'-lanterns?

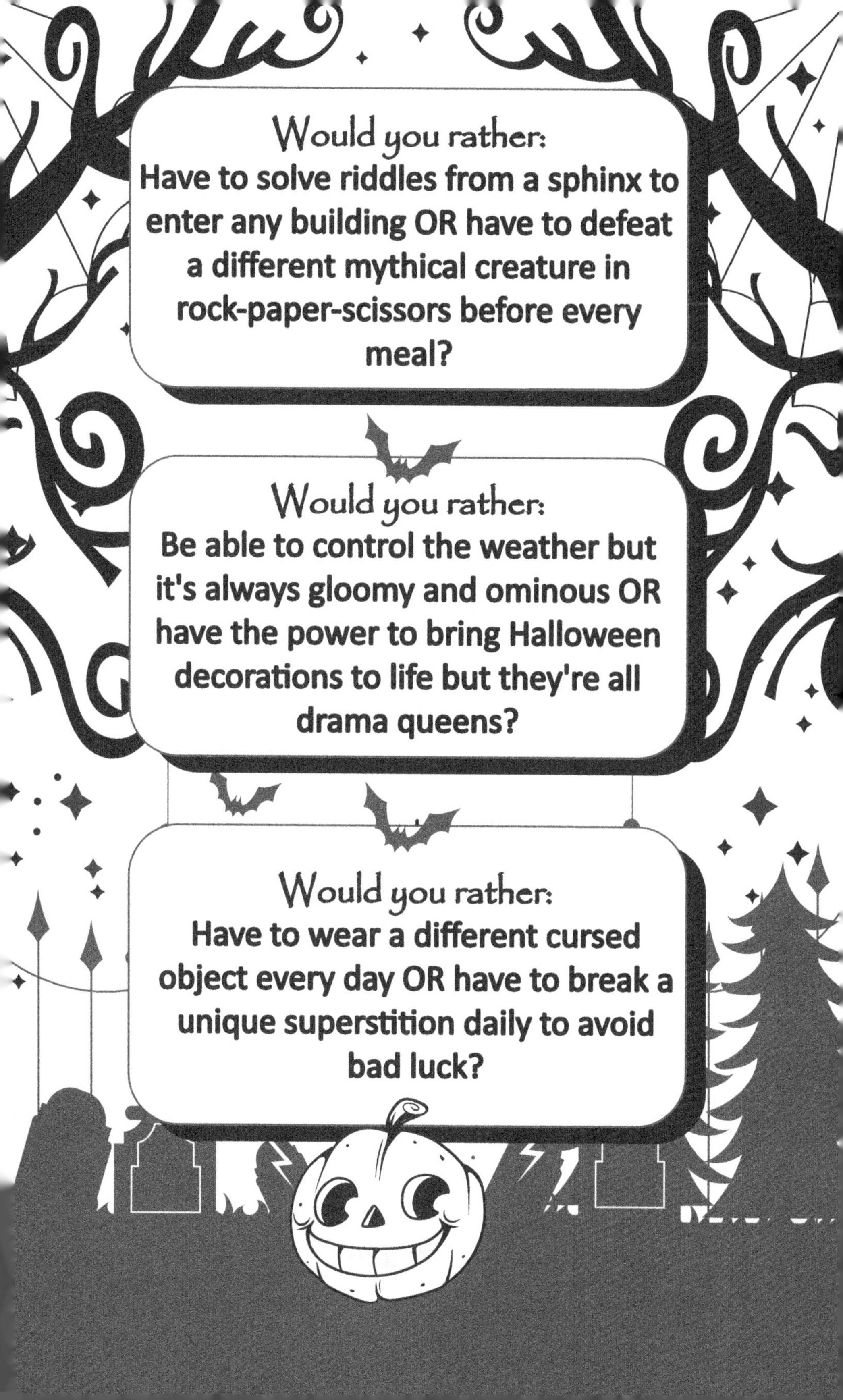

Would you rather:
Have to solve riddles from a sphinx to enter any building OR have to defeat a different mythical creature in rock-paper-scissors before every meal?

Would you rather:
Be able to control the weather but it's always gloomy and ominous OR have the power to bring Halloween decorations to life but they're all drama queens?

Would you rather:
Have to wear a different cursed object every day OR have to break a unique superstition daily to avoid bad luck?

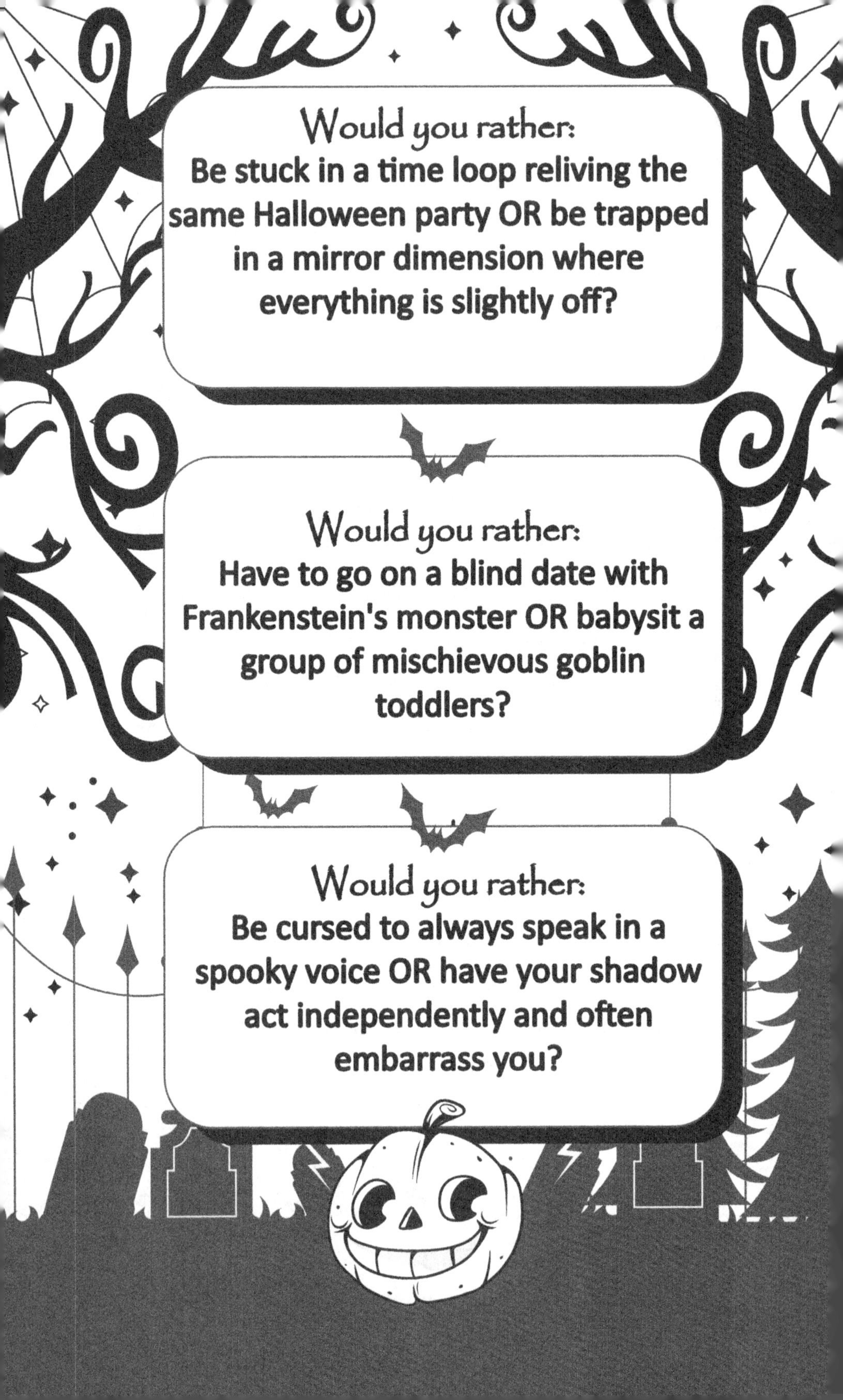

Would you rather:
Be stuck in a time loop reliving the same Halloween party OR be trapped in a mirror dimension where everything is slightly off?

Would you rather:
Have to go on a blind date with Frankenstein's monster OR babysit a group of mischievous goblin toddlers?

Would you rather:
Be cursed to always speak in a spooky voice OR have your shadow act independently and often embarrass you?

Would you rather:
Have a pet black cat that can predict disasters but only through interpretive dance OR a pet raven that can recite poetry but only at 3 AM?

Would you rather:
Be forced to watch every horror movie ever made in one sitting OR have to listen to "Monster Mash" on repeat for a month straight?

Would you rather:
Have the ability to teleport but only to and from cemeteries OR be able to fly but only while wearing a full-body Halloween costume?

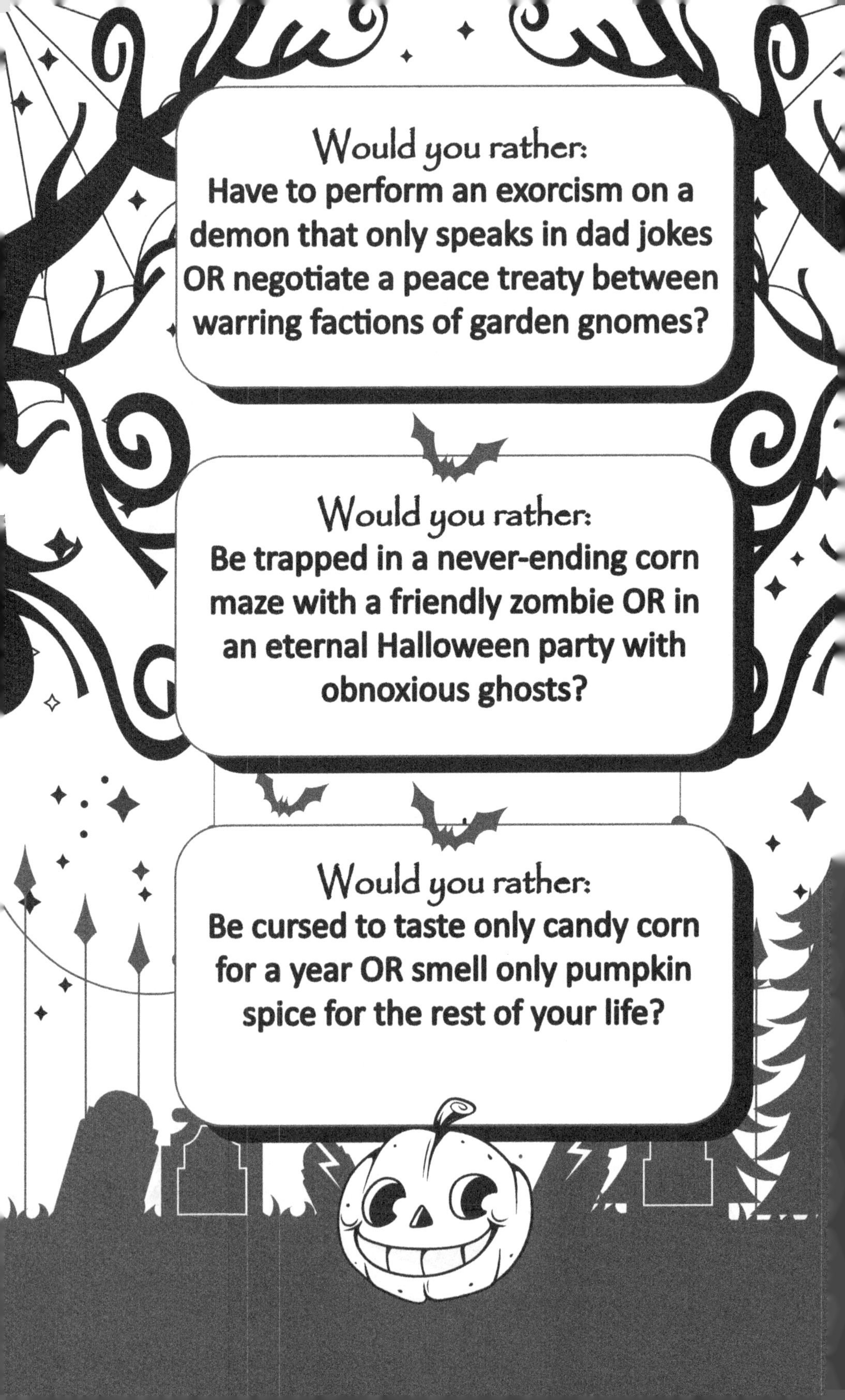
Would you rather:
Have to perform an exorcism on a demon that only speaks in dad jokes OR negotiate a peace treaty between warring factions of garden gnomes?
Would you rather:
Be trapped in a never-ending corn maze with a friendly zombie OR in an eternal Halloween party with obnoxious ghosts?
Would you rather:
Be cursed to taste only candy corn for a year OR smell only pumpkin spice for the rest of your life?

Would you rather:
Have the Headless Horseman
as your Uber driver OR Dracula as
your Airbnb host?
Would you rather:
Be able to shapeshift into any
Halloween decoration OR have the
power to bring any jack-o'-lantern
to life?
Would you rather:
Have to trick-or-treat at real
monsters' houses OR have to give
out candy to monster children
at your door?

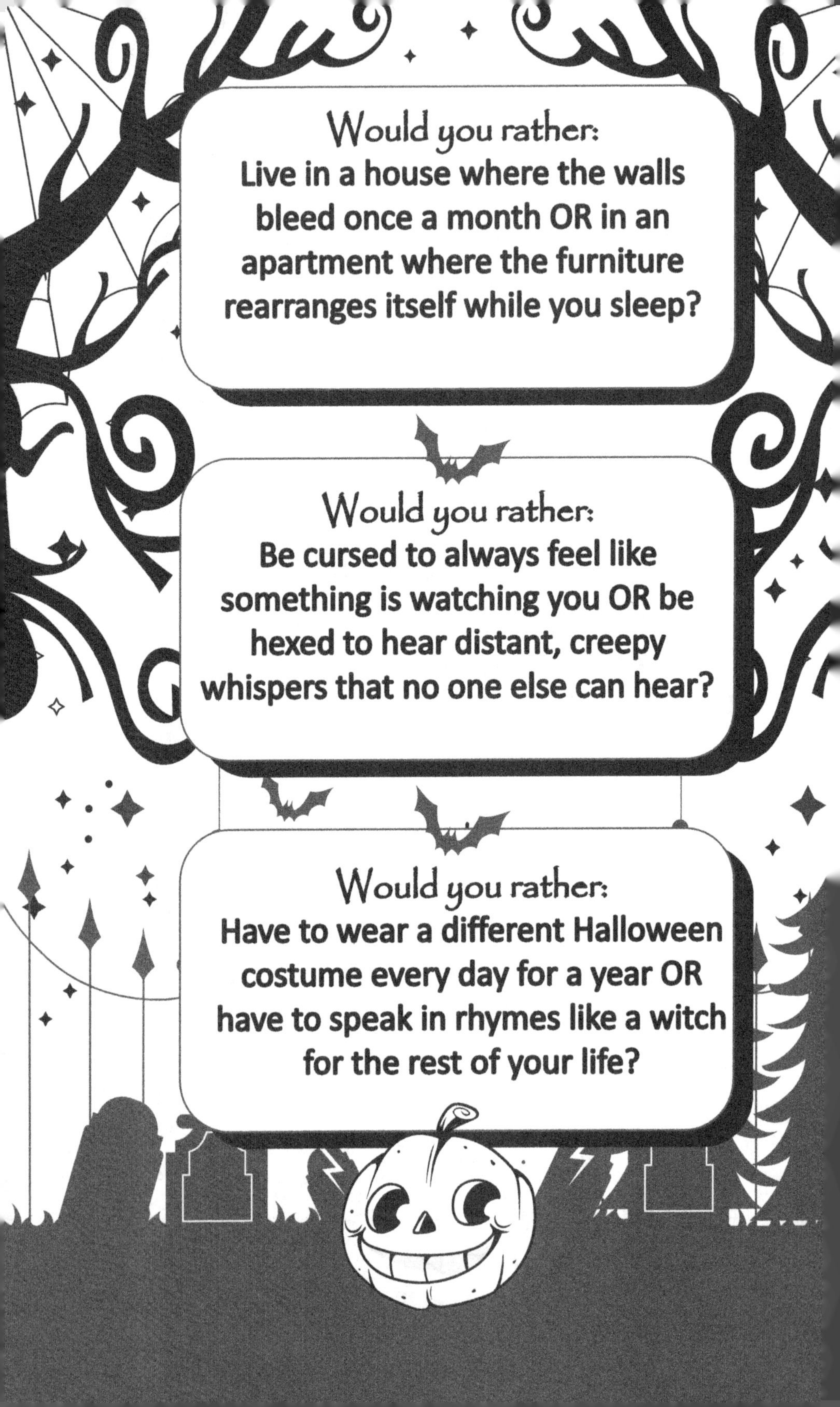
Would you rather:
Live in a house where the walls bleed once a month OR in an apartment where the furniture rearranges itself while you sleep?
Would you rather:
Be cursed to always feel like something is watching you OR be hexed to hear distant, creepy whispers that no one else can hear?
Would you rather:
Have to wear a different Halloween costume every day for a year OR have to speak in rhymes like a witch for the rest of your life?

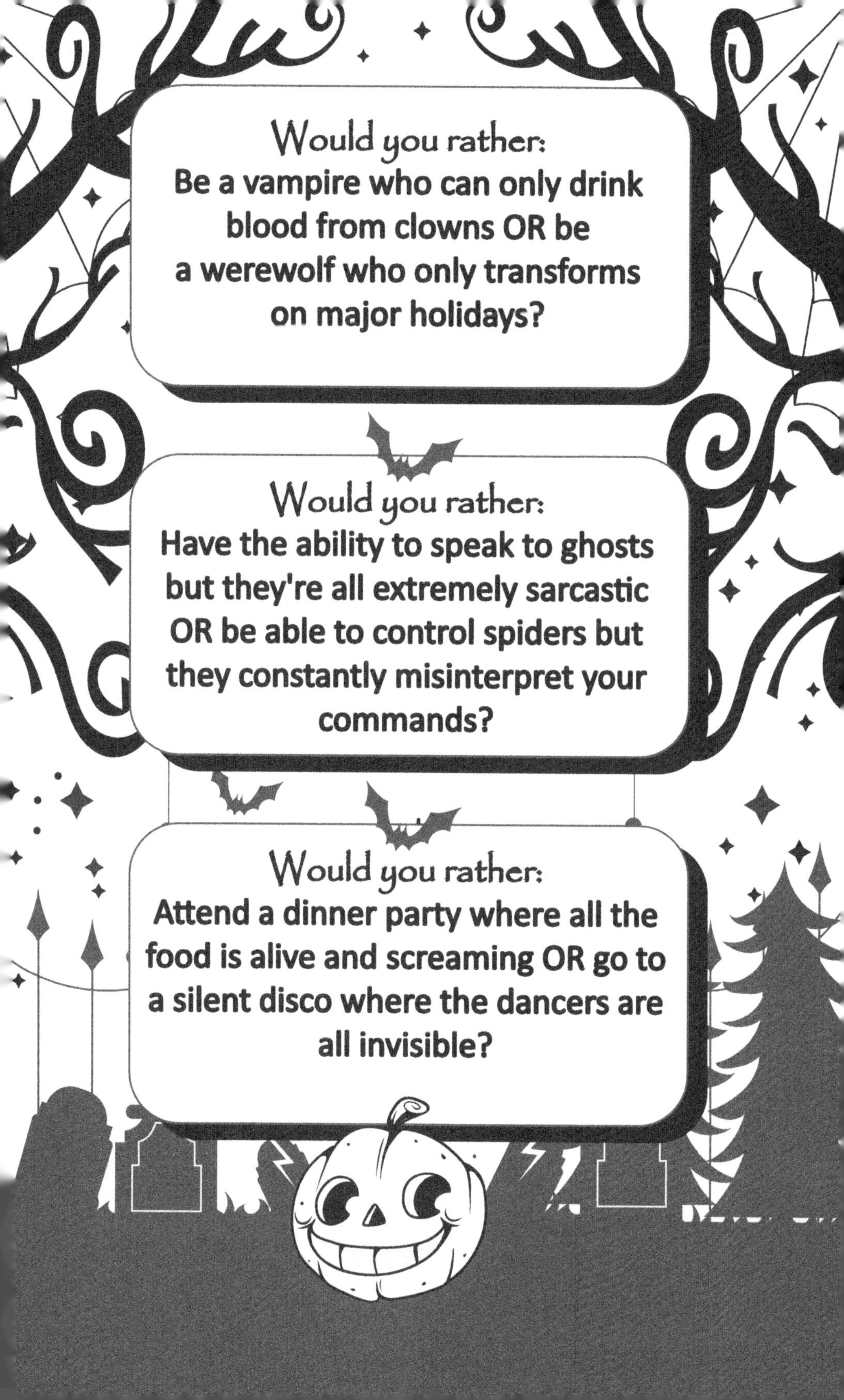
Would you rather:
Be a vampire who can only drink blood from clowns OR be a werewolf who only transforms on major holidays?
Would you rather:
Have the ability to speak to ghosts but they're all extremely sarcastic OR be able to control spiders but they constantly misinterpret your commands?
Would you rather:
Attend a dinner party where all the food is alive and screaming OR go to a silent disco where the dancers are all invisible?

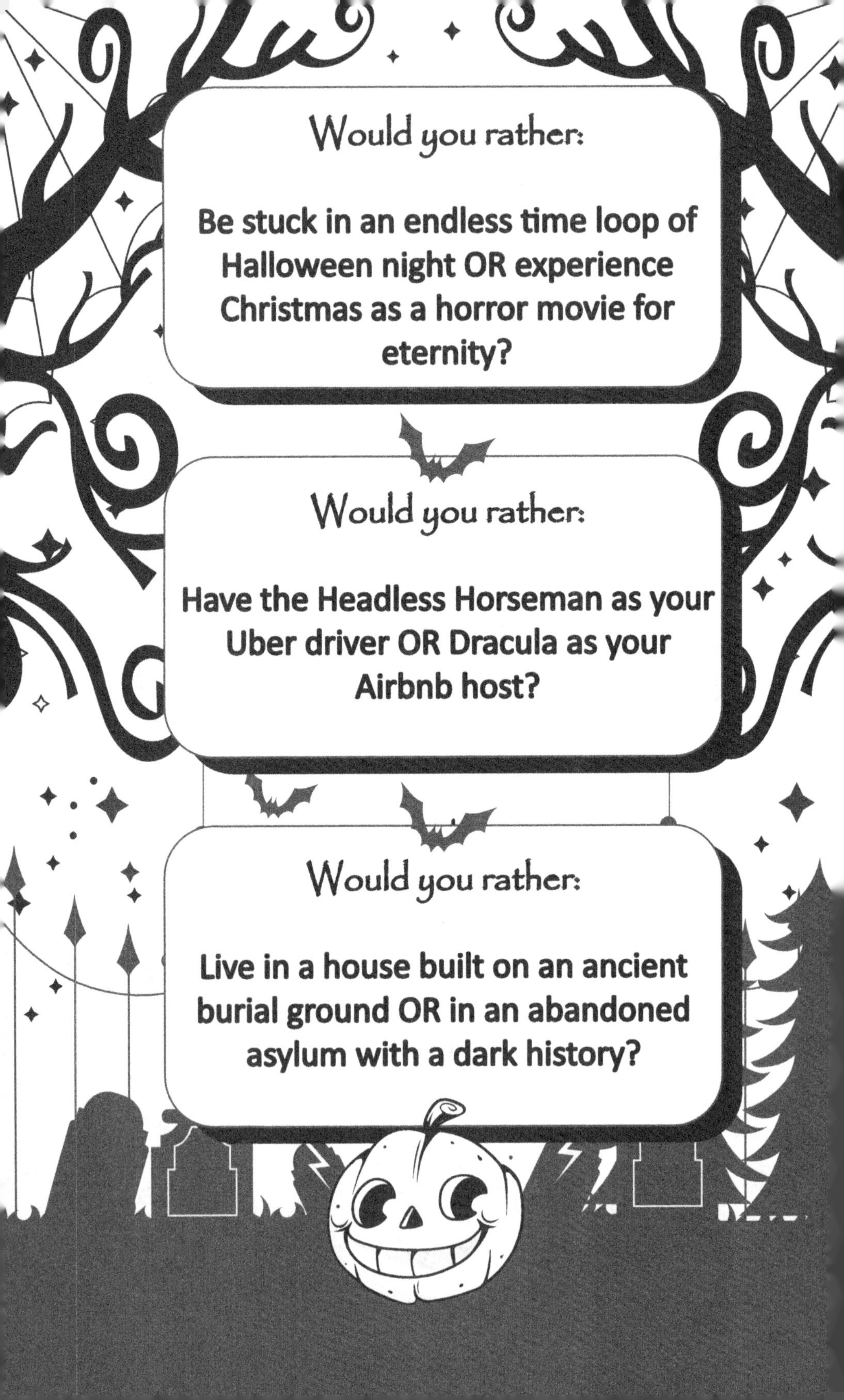

Would you rather:

Be stuck in an endless time loop of Halloween night OR experience Christmas as a horror movie for eternity?

Would you rather:

Have the Headless Horseman as your Uber driver OR Dracula as your Airbnb host?

Would you rather:

Live in a house built on an ancient burial ground OR in an abandoned asylum with a dark history?

What do you call a skeleton who won't work?
Lazy bones!
What do you call a vampire's favorite fruit?
A bloody orange!
What do you call a witch's garage?
A broom closet!

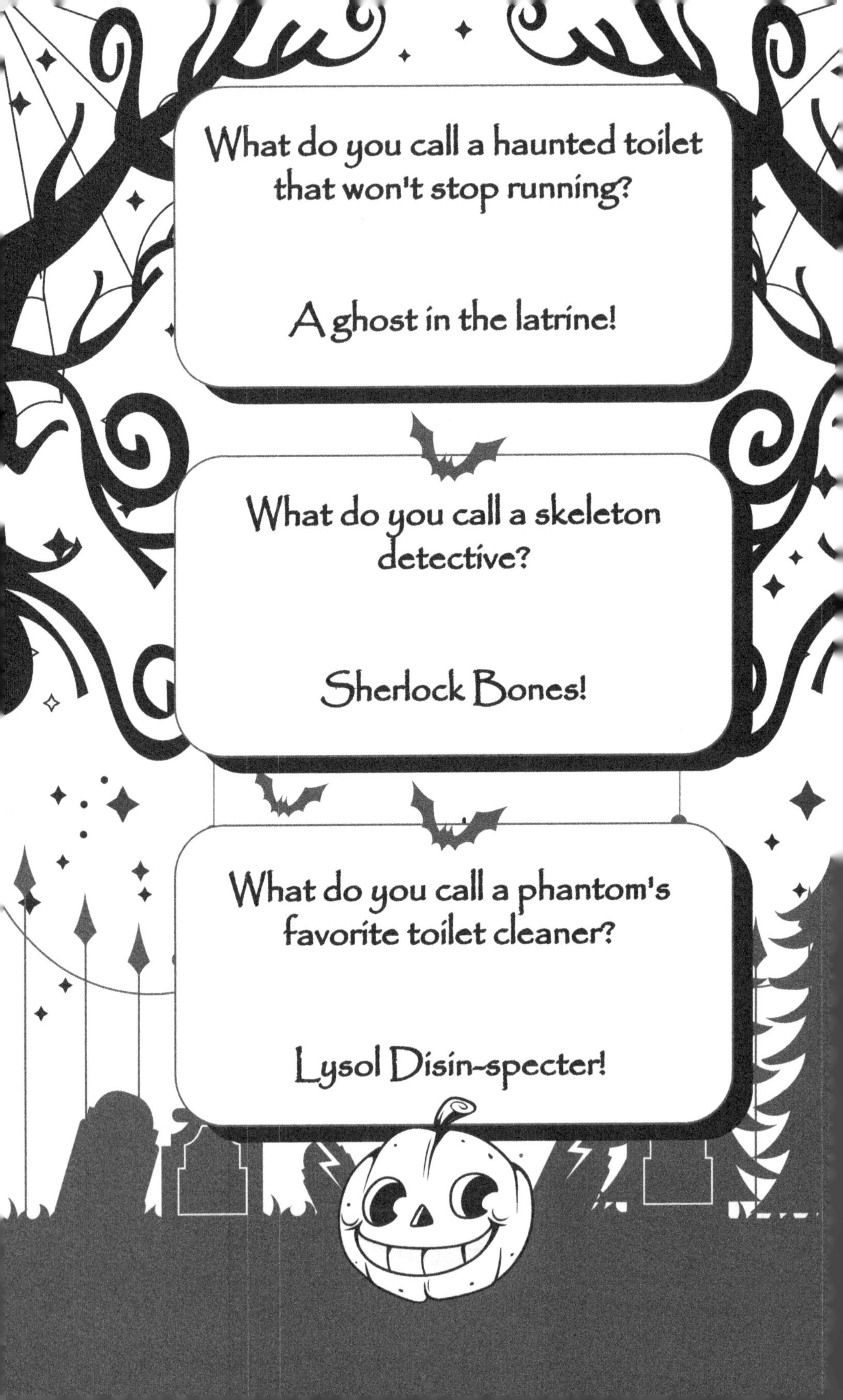

What do you call a haunted toilet that won't stop running?

A ghost in the latrine!

What do you call a skeleton detective?

Sherlock Bones!

What do you call a phantom's favorite toilet cleaner?

Lysol Disin-specter!

Why did the ghost refuse to use the port-a-potty?
It wasn't his type of sheet!
What do you call a mummy's dog?
Anubiscuit.
What do you call a lazy kangaroo?
A pouch potato!

Why did the headless horseman go into business?

He heard he was going places!

Why did the jack-o'-lantern blush?

Because he saw the salad dressing!

Why did the mummy bring a sewing kit to the bathroom?

In case of a wrap malfunction!

What do you get when you cross Bambi with a ghost?
Bamboo!
What do you say to comfort a crying mummy? "
Quit your tomb-ing!"
Why did the mummy bring a first aid kit to the bathroom?
In case of emergency un-wrapping!

What do you get from a pampered cow?

Spoiled milk!

What do you call it when a ghost possesses a mime?

Silent but deadly!

What do you call an owl that's seen a ghost?

Terrified.

What do you call a ghost's favorite bathroom fixture?

A boo-det!

What do you call a ghost's favorite type of dance?

The ghost tango!

What do you call a ghost's favorite laxative?

Casper oil!

What do ghosts use to wipe?
Sheet paper!
What do ghosts use to fix leaky toilets?
Spook-tite!
What do ghosts use to clean their toilet bowls?
Scrubbing boo-bles!

What did the ghost teacher say to the class?
"Look at me when I'm talking to you...BOO!"
What do ghosts use to unclog their toilets?
A poo-tergeist!
What do mummies use instead of toilet paper?
Wrap-kins!

What did the ghost say after eating too much candy corn?

"I've got a bad case of the boo-belly!"

I tried to train my cat to detect ghost poop. Now he just stares at empty litter boxes for hours.

I tried to start a shit-talking club, but it was a crap idea.

I tried to create a ghost poop detector. It kept going off every time I had gas.

I tried to create a ghost poop detector. It kept going off every time I had gas.

I tried to make a poop emoji costume, but it was a crappy attempt.

I started a ghost poop collection. My family thinks I'm just full of hot air.

Ghost poop is the reason why some toilets are always cold. They're trying to provide a cozy home for spectral specimens.

I heard ghost poop is actually ectoplasm. That explains why my bathroom always feels slimed.

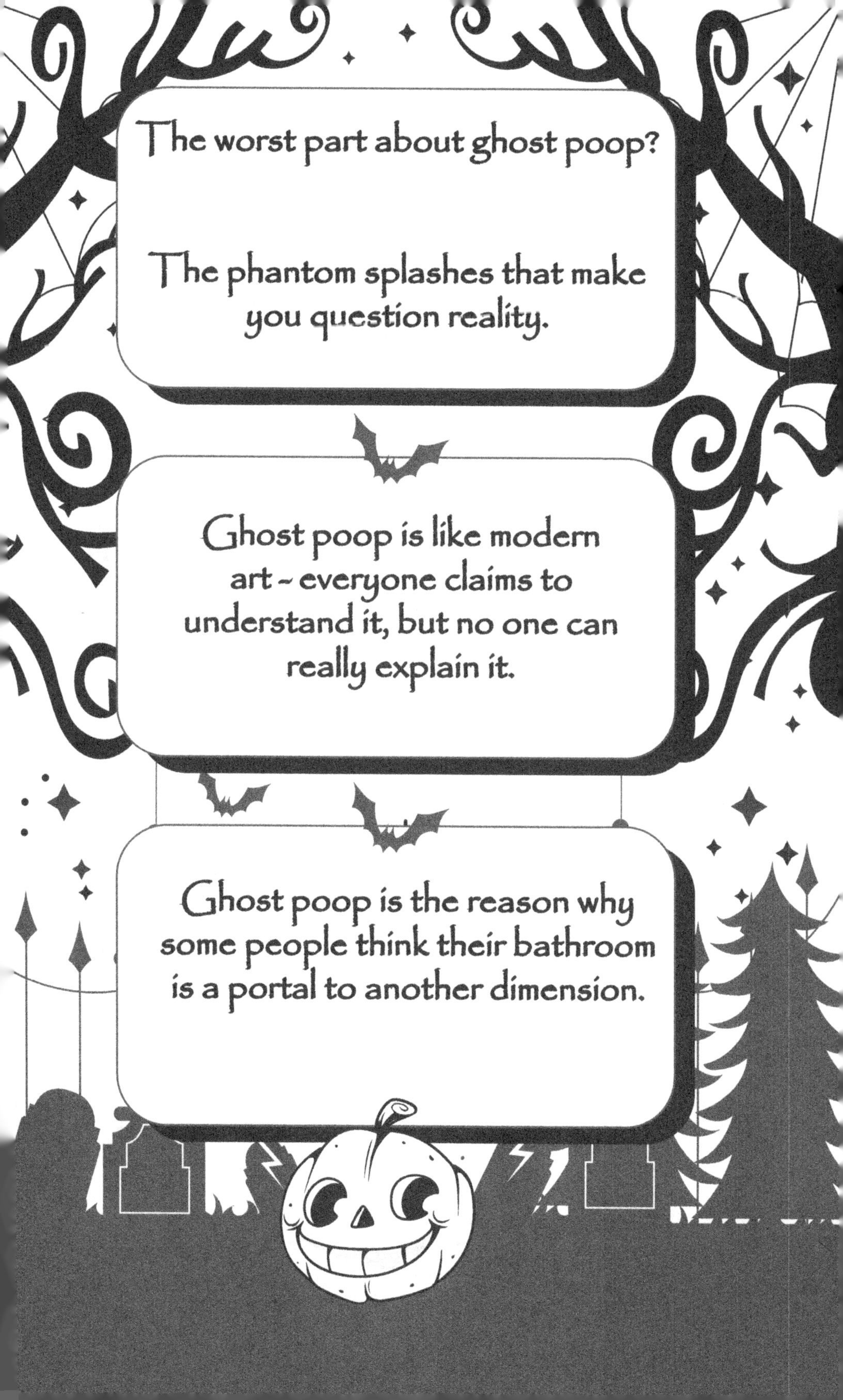
The worst part about ghost poop?
The phantom splashes that make you question reality.
Ghost poop is like modern art - everyone claims to understand it, but no one can really explain it.
Ghost poop is the reason why some people think their bathroom is a portal to another dimension.

The hardest part of being a ghost?

Explaining to other ghosts why you're sitting on a toilet.

The Ghostbusters' least popular spin-off?

Ghost Pooper Busters. They just couldn't capture the essence of the original.

The best thing about ghost poop?

No skid marks on your underwear.

The problem with ghost poop is that it's always invisible to the naked eye. Talk about a spectral specimen!
What's a vampire's favorite kind of dog?
A bloodhound!
What's a vampire's favorite ship?
A blood vessel!

What's a vampire's favorite toilet paper brand?
Quilted Northern Fright!
What's a vampire's favorite type of music?
Bach-lover music!
What's a vampire's favorite type of toilet?
A blood bowl!

What's a vampire's least favorite bathroom fixture?

The cross-shaped faucet handles!

What's a vampire's least favorite bathroom accessory?

Garlic-scented candles!

What's a vampire's idea of a perfect bathroom?

One with bloody good plumbing!

What's a werewolf's least favorite bathroom cleaner?

Silver polish!

What's a witch's favorite type of toilet?

A caul-dron!

Why don't ghosts need to worry about clogged toilets?

Everything passes right through them!

Why don't ghosts need to flush?
Their business disappears into thin air!
Why don't ghosts need to buy toilet brush refills?
Their old ones last for an eternity!
Why don't ghosts need to buy new toilets?
They can always use their old ones in the after-life!

Why did the zombie skip dessert?

He only had room for one brain.

Why didn't the skeleton cross the road?

Because he had no guts!

Why do skeletons love rollercoasters?

They give them a spine-tingling good time!

Why did the zombie refuse to use the bathroom?

He was afraid he'd fall apart!

Why don't mummies need to worry about toilet seat warmers?

They're always wrapped up warm!

Why don't skeletons go to parties?

They have no body to dance with!

Why don't zombies worry about toilet paper shortages?
They're used to wiping with their own flaking skin!
Why don't zombies use toilet paper?
They prefer to use their own dead skin!
Why don't skeletons like spicy food?
It goes right through them!

Why don't zombies worry about toilet paper splinters?
They're already falling apart!
Why is Dracula so unpopular?
He's a real pain in the neck!
Why was the skeleton afraid to use the haunted outhouse?
He didn't have the guts!

Why did the ghost bring a fan to the bathroom?
He wanted to create a paranormal activity!
What's the difference between a ghost and a pizza?
You can't order a ghost with extra cheese!
What's a zombie's idea of a toilet freshener?
Eau de decay!

Where do cool ghosts hang out?
Day-care centers!
Where does Dracula keep his money?
In a blood bank!
Why are ghosts such bad liars?
Because you can see right through them!

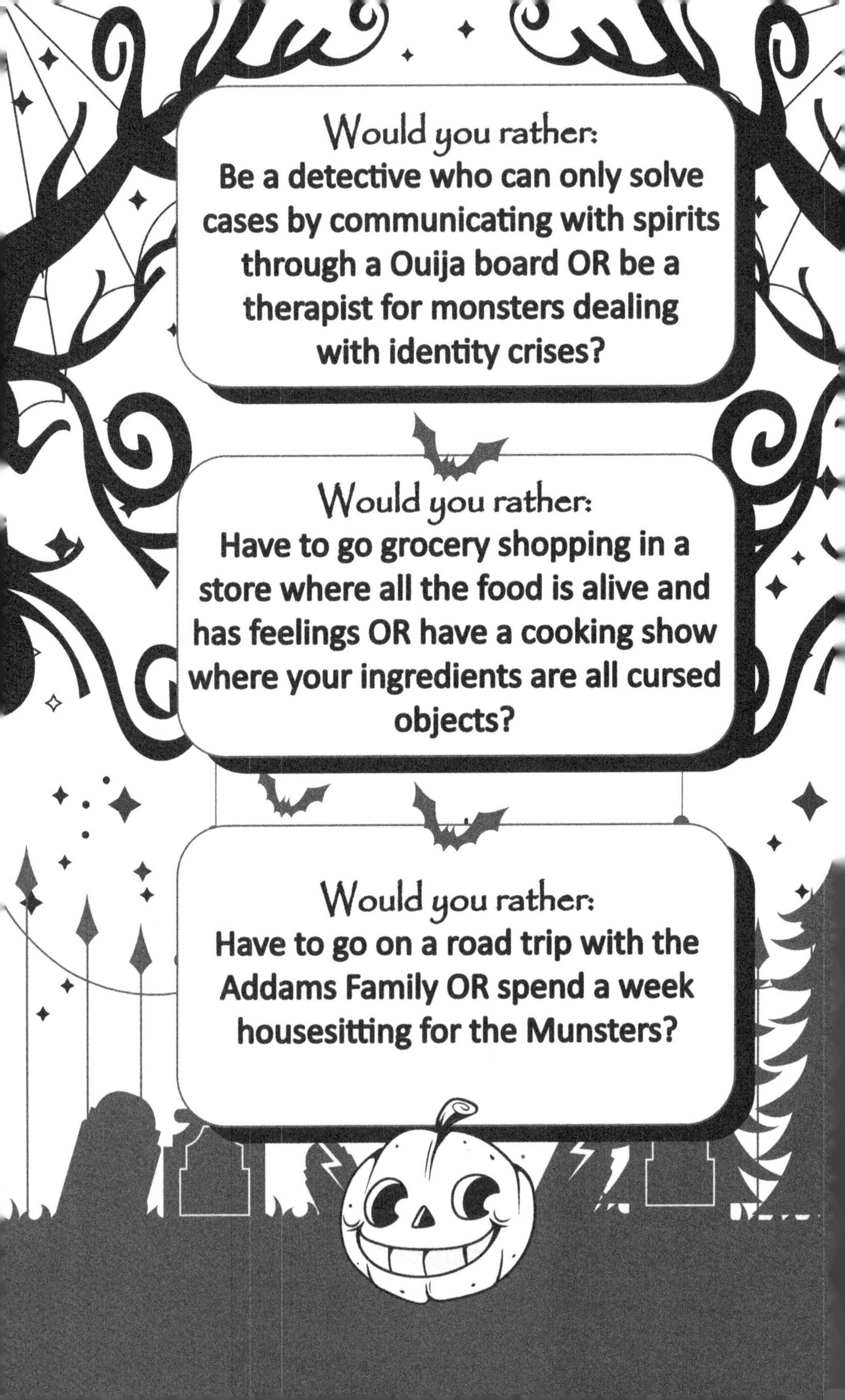

Would you rather:

Be a detective who can only solve cases by communicating with spirits through a Ouija board OR be a therapist for monsters dealing with identity crises?

Would you rather:

Have to go grocery shopping in a store where all the food is alive and has feelings OR have a cooking show where your ingredients are all cursed objects?

Would you rather:

Have to go on a road trip with the Addams Family OR spend a week housesitting for the Munsters?

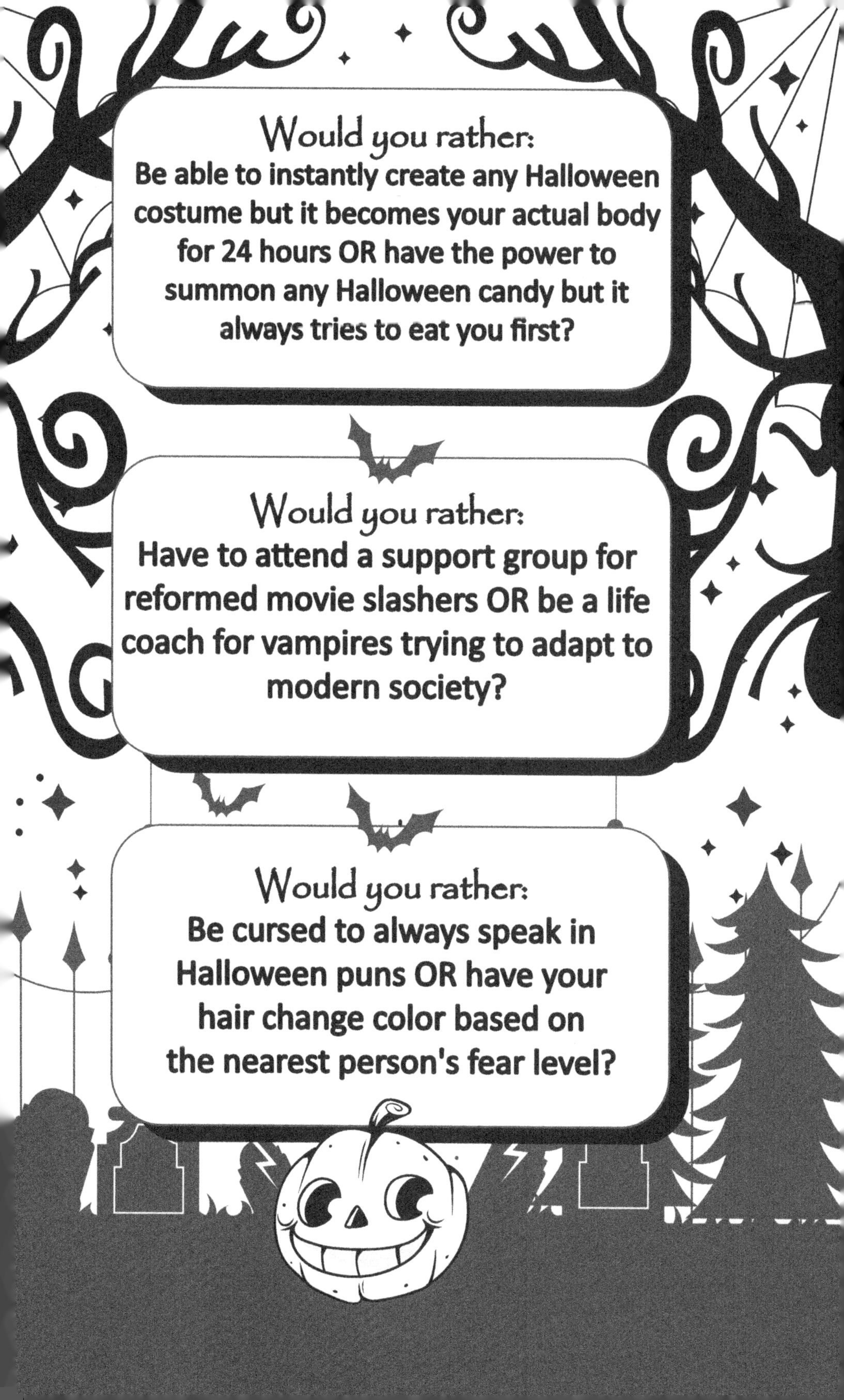

Would you rather:

Be able to instantly create any Halloween costume but it becomes your actual body for 24 hours OR have the power to summon any Halloween candy but it always tries to eat you first?

Would you rather:

Have to attend a support group for reformed movie slashers OR be a life coach for vampires trying to adapt to modern society?

Would you rather:

Be cursed to always speak in Halloween puns OR have your hair change color based on the nearest person's fear level?

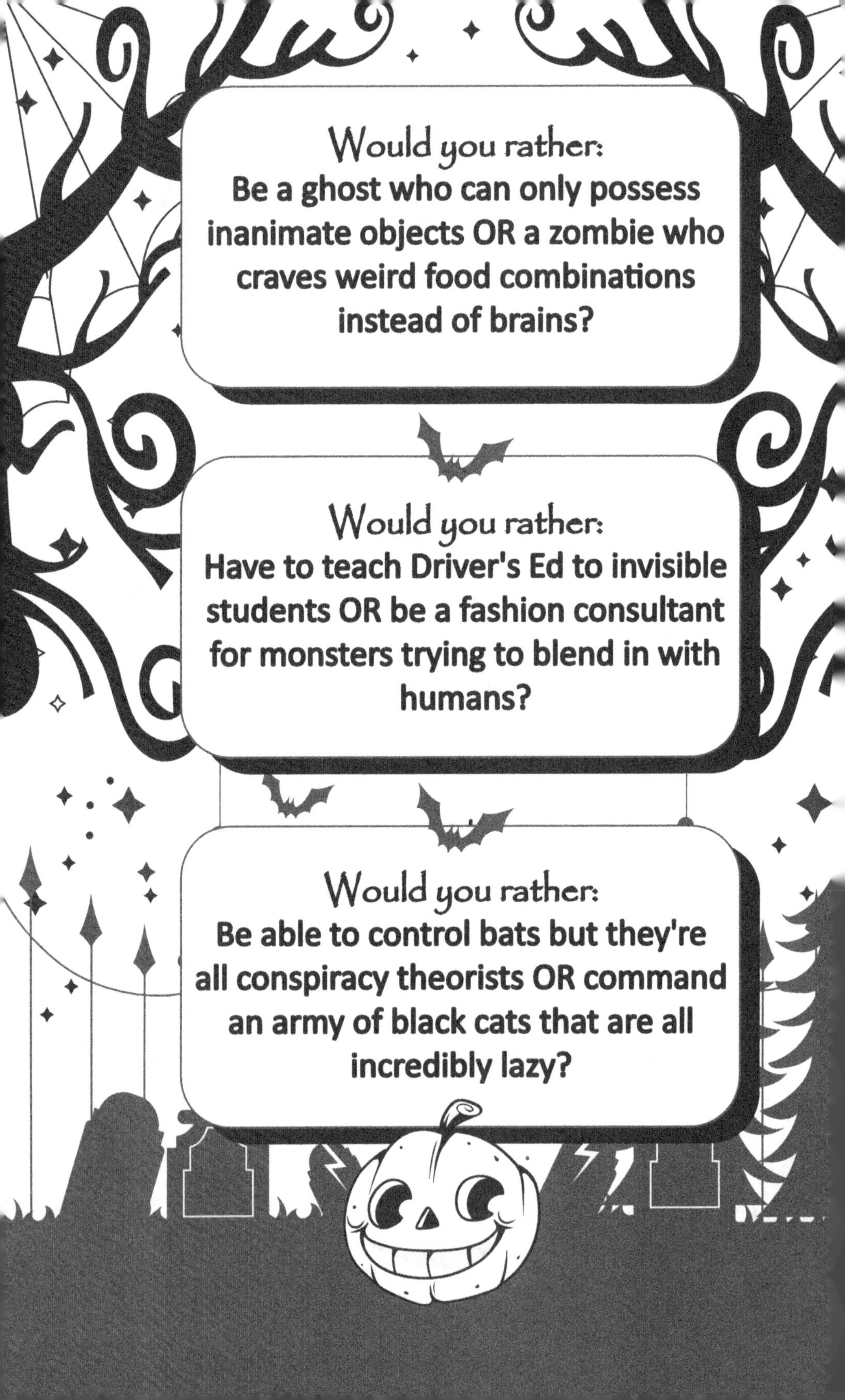

Would you rather:
Be a ghost who can only possess inanimate objects OR a zombie who craves weird food combinations instead of brains?

Would you rather:
Have to teach Driver's Ed to invisible students OR be a fashion consultant for monsters trying to blend in with humans?

Would you rather:
Be able to control bats but they're all conspiracy theorists OR command an army of black cats that are all incredibly lazy?

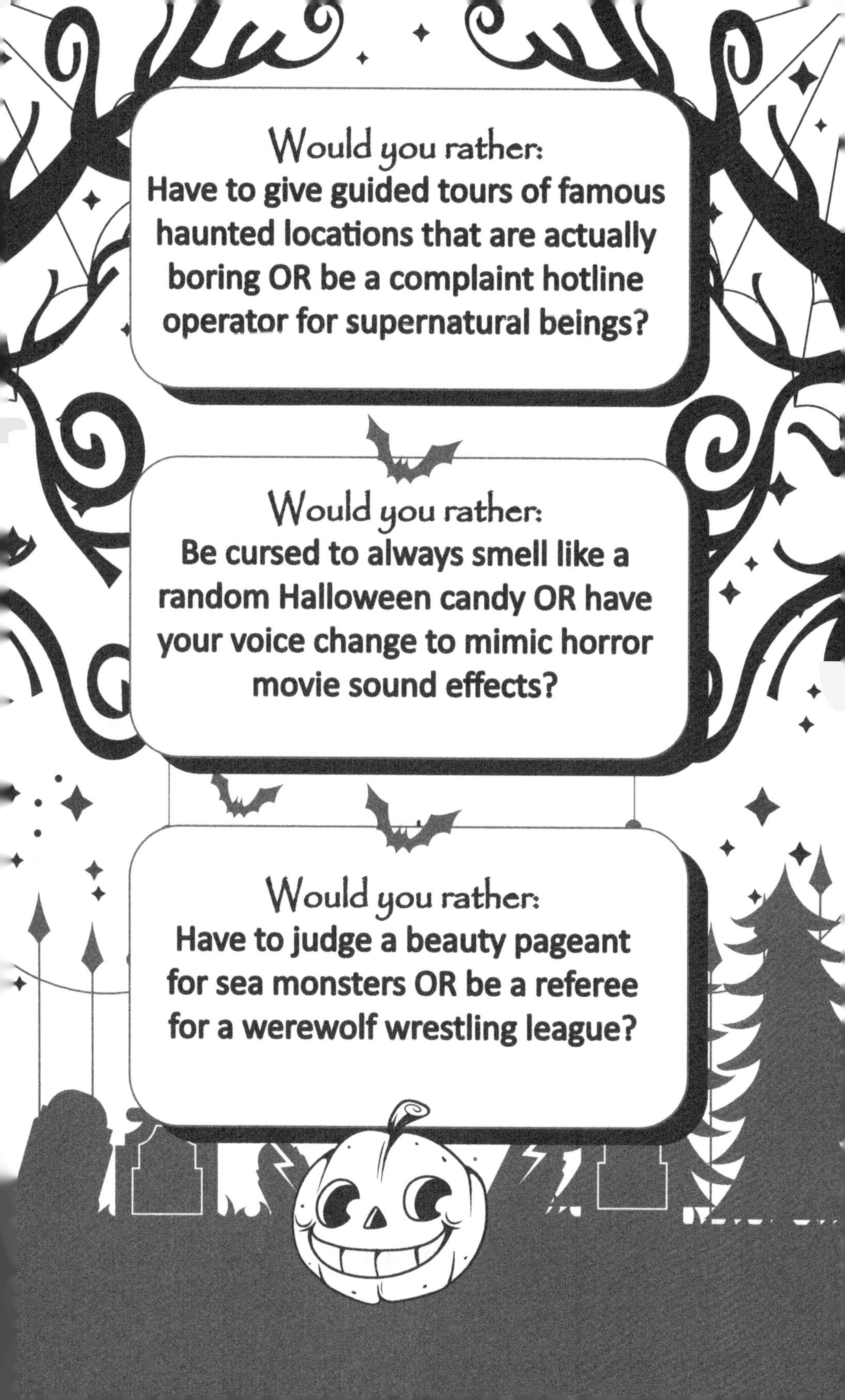

Would you rather:
Have to give guided tours of famous haunted locations that are actually boring OR be a complaint hotline operator for supernatural beings?

Would you rather:
Be cursed to always smell like a random Halloween candy OR have your voice change to mimic horror movie sound effects?

Would you rather:
Have to judge a beauty pageant for sea monsters OR be a referee for a werewolf wrestling league?

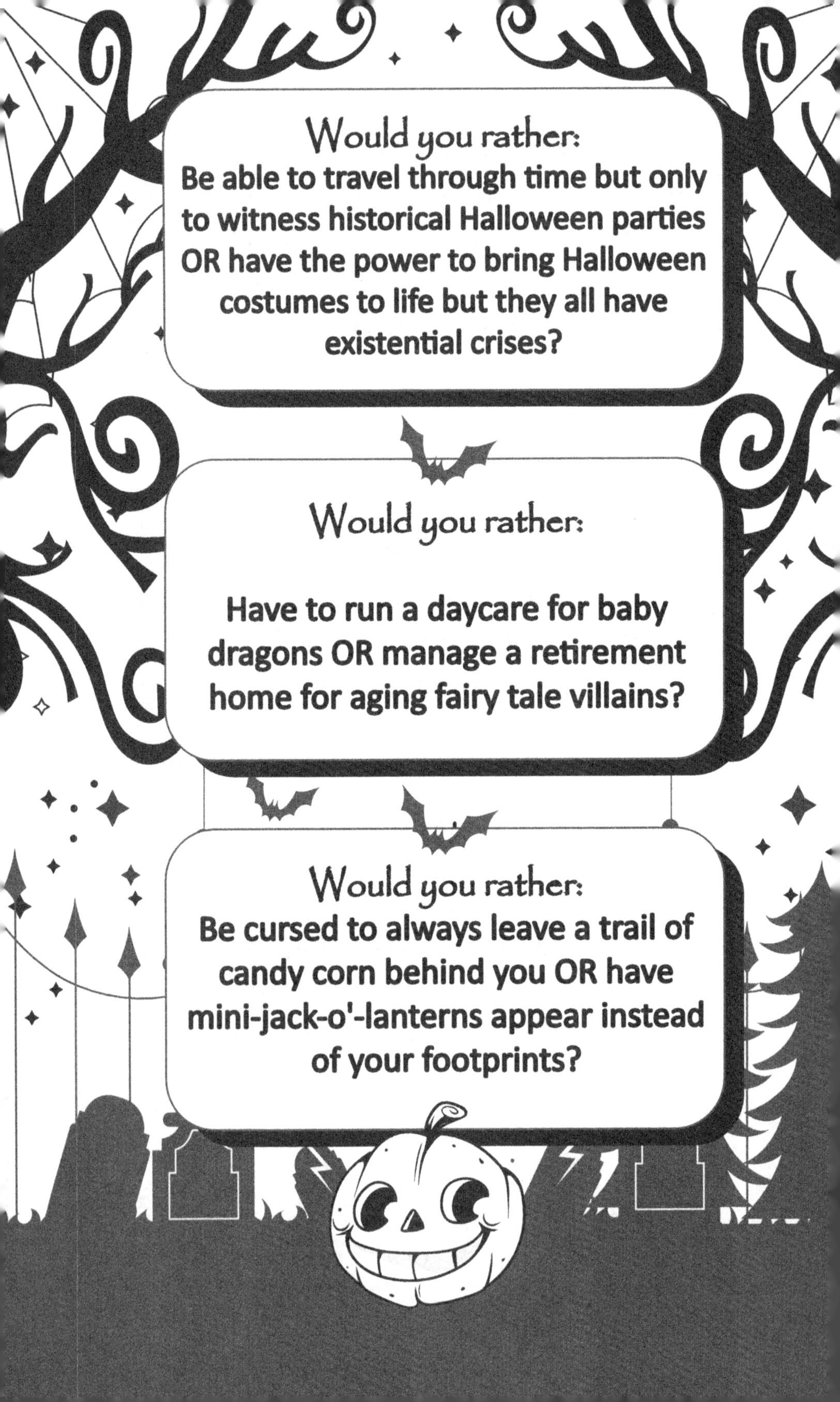

Would you rather:
Be able to travel through time but only to witness historical Halloween parties OR have the power to bring Halloween costumes to life but they all have existential crises?

Would you rather:

Have to run a daycare for baby dragons OR manage a retirement home for aging fairy tale villains?

Would you rather:
Be cursed to always leave a trail of candy corn behind you OR have mini-jack-o'-lanterns appear instead of your footprints?

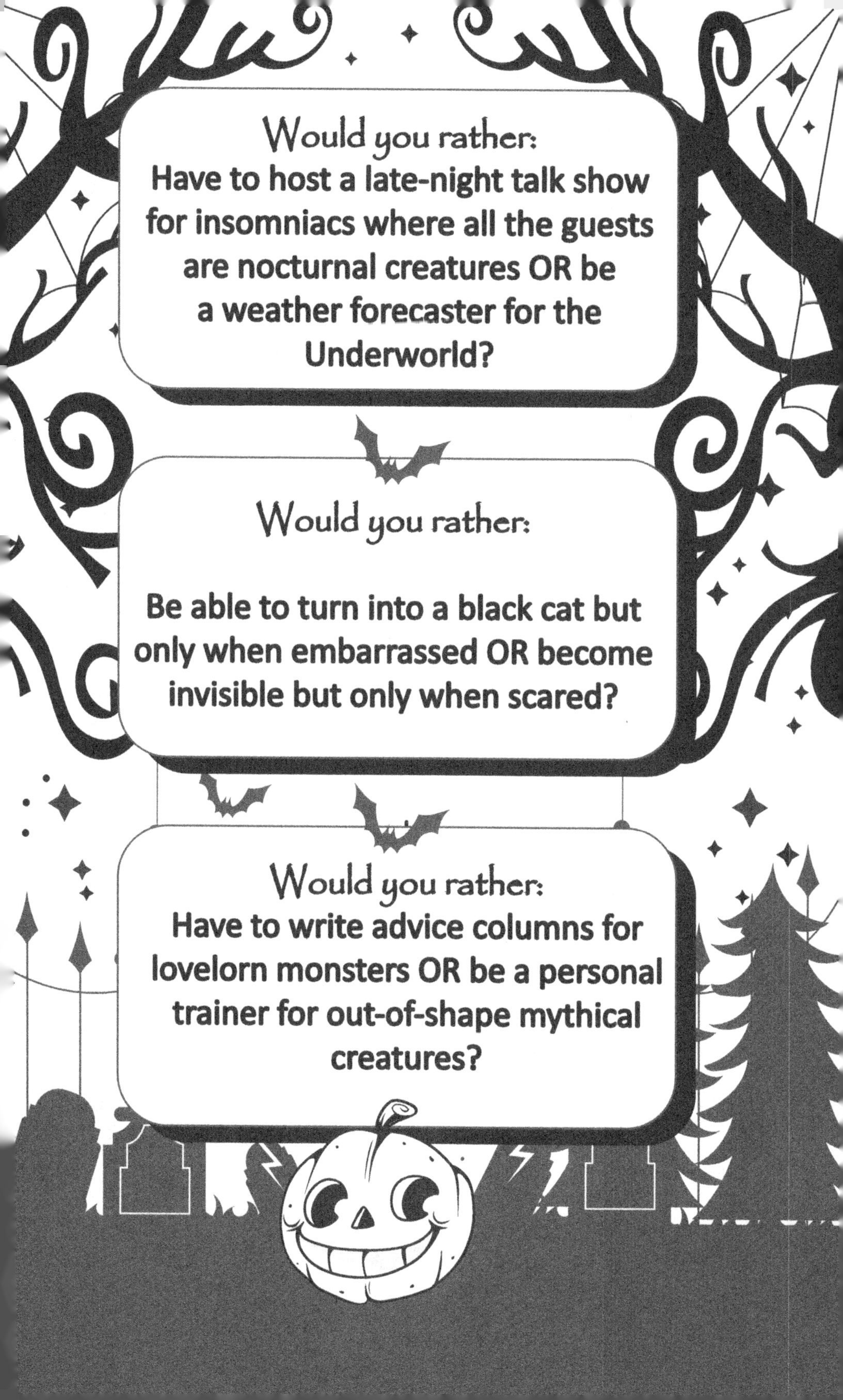

Would you rather:
Have to host a late-night talk show for insomniacs where all the guests are nocturnal creatures OR be a weather forecaster for the Underworld?

Would you rather:

Be able to turn into a black cat but only when embarrassed OR become invisible but only when scared?

Would you rather:
Have to write advice columns for lovelorn monsters OR be a personal trainer for out-of-shape mythical creatures?

Would you rather:
Be able to conjure any Halloween decoration but it appears in the least convenient place OR have the power to instantly change into any costume but you can't control what it will be?
Would you rather:
Have to organize speed dating events for classic movie monsters OR be a couples counselor for dysfunctional supernatural pairs?
Would you rather:
Be cursed to speak only in ghostly moans and wails OR have skeleton hands that play xylophone tunes whenever you move them?

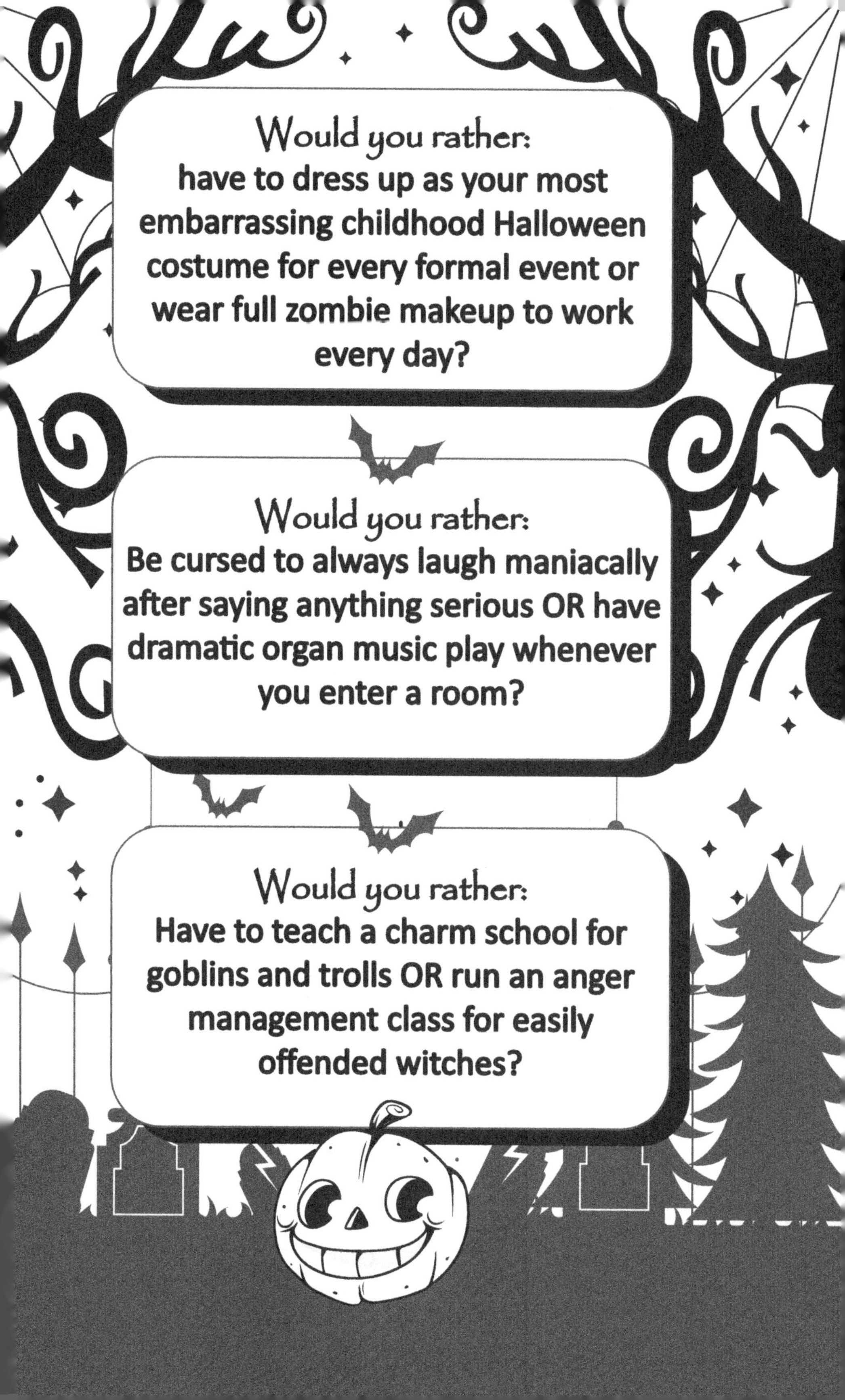
Would you rather:
have to dress up as your most embarrassing childhood Halloween costume for every formal event or wear full zombie makeup to work every day?
Would you rather:
Be cursed to always laugh maniacally after saying anything serious OR have dramatic organ music play whenever you enter a room?
Would you rather:
Have to teach a charm school for goblins and trolls OR run an anger management class for easily offended witches?

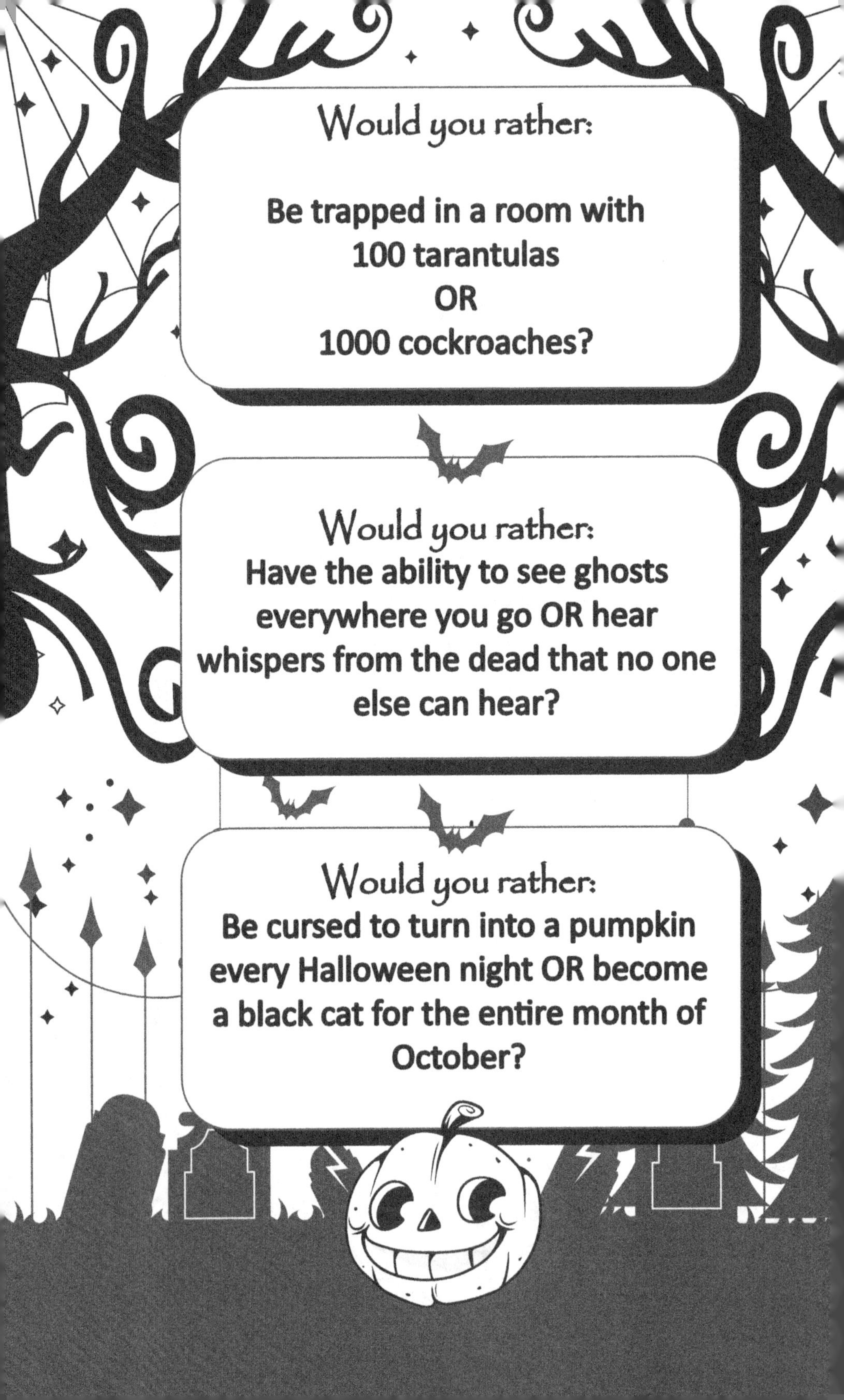

Would you rather:
Be trapped in a room with
100 tarantulas
OR
1000 cockroaches?
Would you rather:
Have the ability to see ghosts
everywhere you go OR hear
whispers from the dead that no one
else can hear?
Would you rather:
Be cursed to turn into a pumpkin
every Halloween night OR become
a black cat for the entire month of
October?

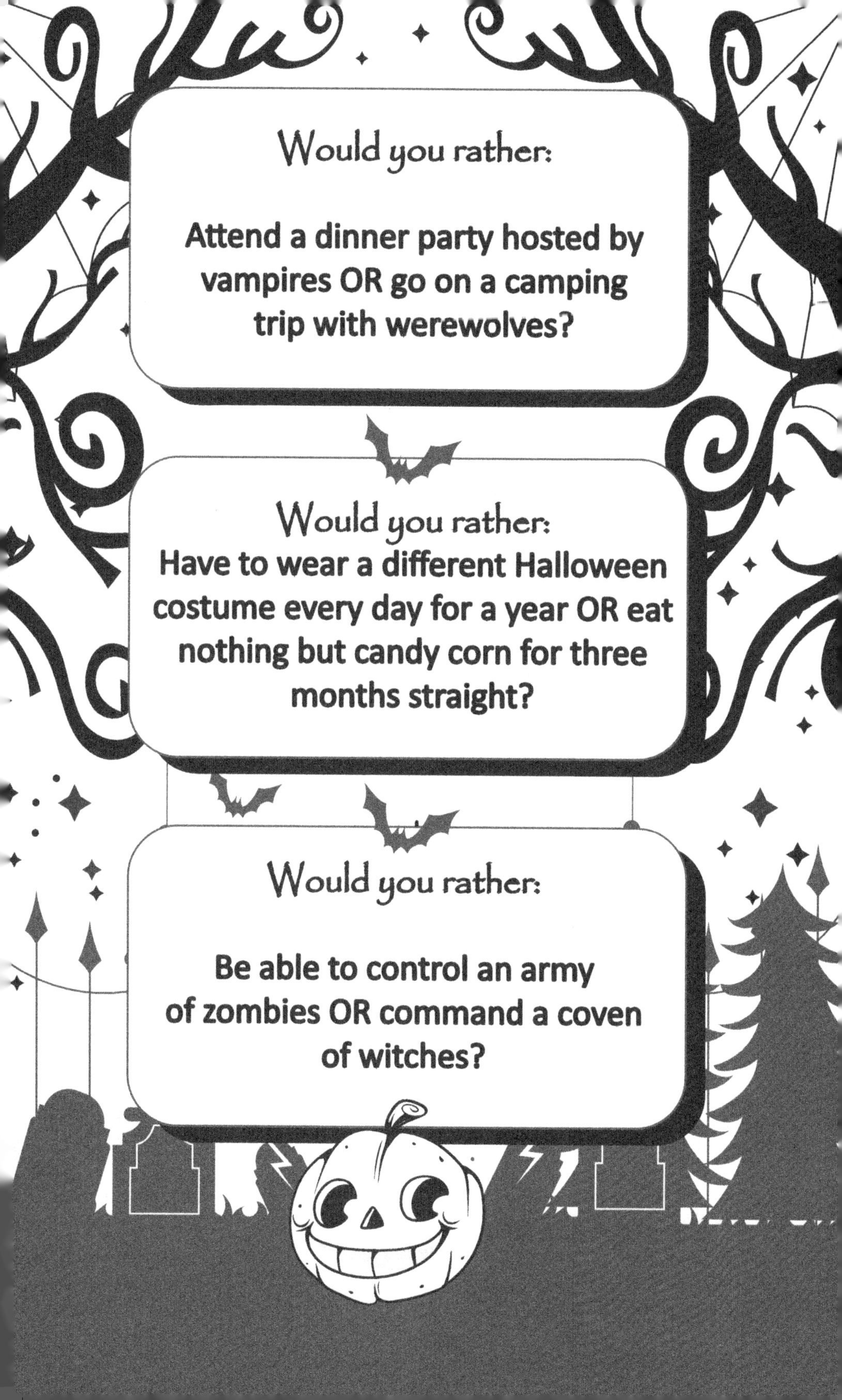
Would you rather:
Attend a dinner party hosted by vampires OR go on a camping trip with werewolves?
Would you rather:
Have to wear a different Halloween costume every day for a year OR eat nothing but candy corn for three months straight?
Would you rather:
Be able to control an army of zombies OR command a coven of witches?

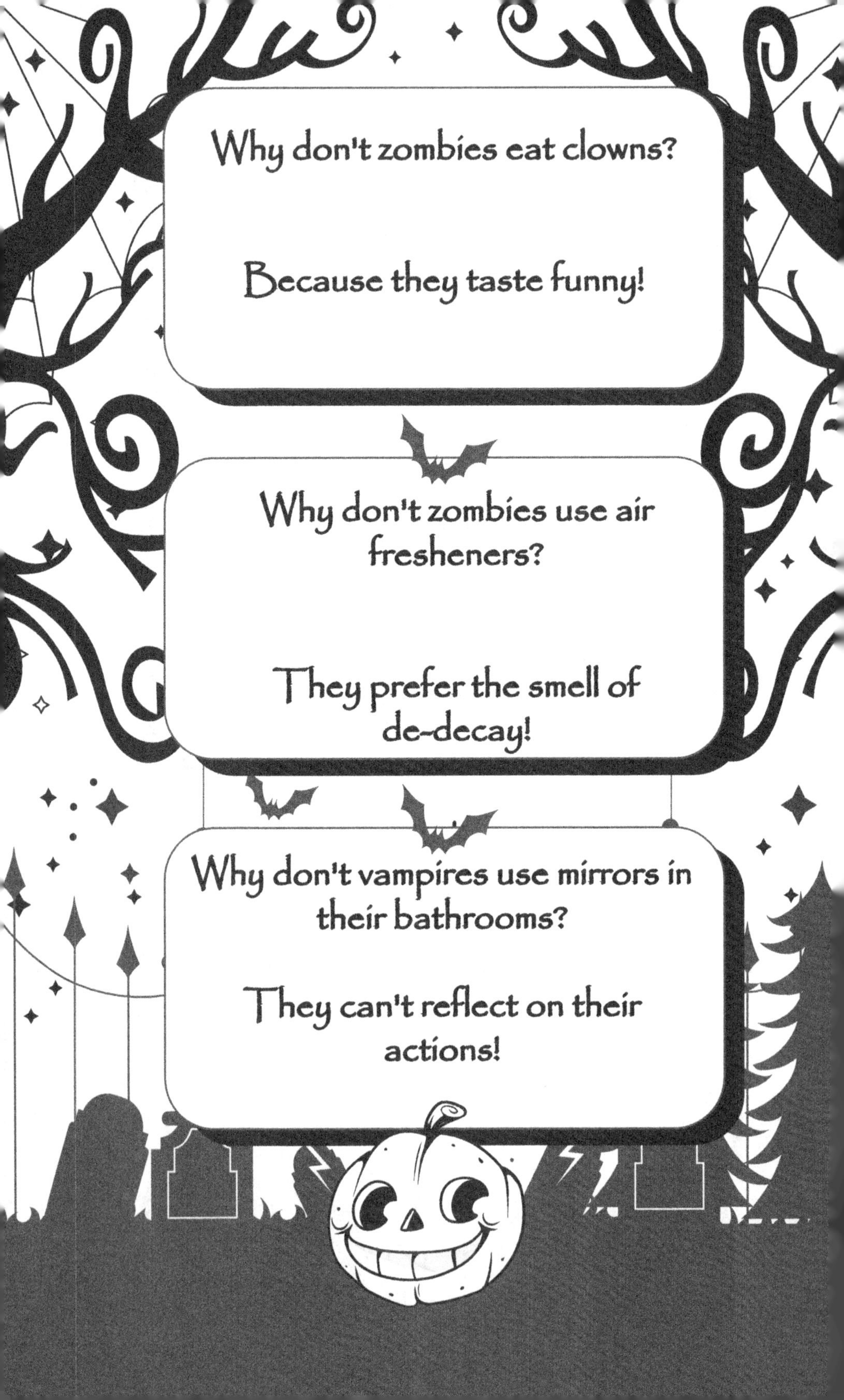

Why don't zombies eat clowns?

Because they taste funny!

Why don't zombies use air fresheners?

They prefer the smell of de-decay!

Why don't vampires use mirrors in their bathrooms?

They can't reflect on their actions!

Why don't skeletons use scented toilet paper?
They've lost their sense of smell!
Why don't skeletons use toilet seat covers?
They've got nothing to lose!
Why don't they play poker in the haunted house?
Too many cheaters!

Why don't skeletons fight each other?
They don't have the guts.
Why don't skeletons ever go trick-or-treating?
Because they have no body to go with!
Why don't mummies need to flush?
They're already preserved!

Why did the vampire bring toilet paper to the party?

He wanted to be the life of the potty!

Why did the vampire become a urologist?

He was interested in bladder control!

Why did the vampire become a plumber?

He was good at dealing with bat-hroom issues!

What do you call a witch who lives at the beach?
A sand-witch!
What do you call a werewolf's least favorite part of the bathroom?
The silver-plated mirror!
What do you call a werewolf with diarrhea?
A poopy puppy!

The worst thing about ghost poop?
The phantom wipes that never end.
I tried to photograph ghost poop with a thermal camera.
All I captured was my own embarrassment.
What does a ghost use to surf the internet?
A scare-ow-are!!

I tried to explain ghost poop to my doctor. Now I have a referral to a gastroenterologist and a psychiatrist.
Why don't mummies need to buy toilet paper?
They're on a roll!
Why did the zombie bring a shovel to the bathroom?
Old habits die hard!

Why did the ghost bring a thermometer to the bathroom?
To check for paranormal activity!
Why did the ghost cross the road?
To get to the other side... and then to haunt the house on the other side!
Why did the ghost get a bad grade in school?
He couldn't see the work!

Why did the ghost bring a thermometer to the bathroom?

To check for paranormal activity!

Why did the ghost get a job at the haunted house?

He was already dead!

Why did the ghost get a job at the library?

He was good at reading between the lines!

What do you call a pumpkin that works at the beach?

A life-gourd.

Why did the pumpkin lose the boxing match?

It didn't have the gourds.

What do you get when you drop a pumpkin?

Squash.

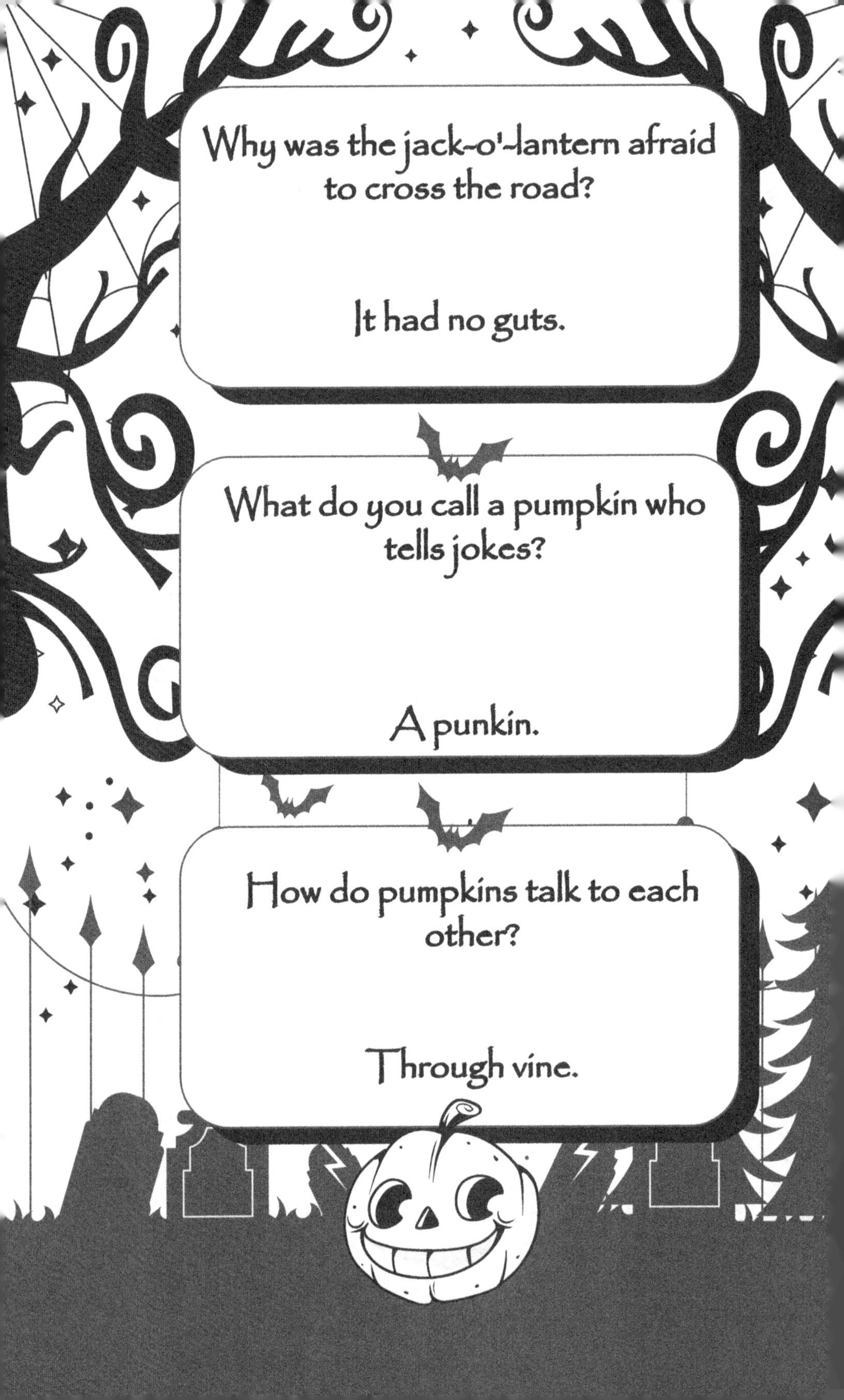

Why was the jack-o'-lantern afraid to cross the road?

It had no guts.

What do you call a pumpkin who tells jokes?

A punkin.

How do pumpkins talk to each other?

Through vine.

What do you call a pumpkin that's really into working out?
A jacked-o'-lantern.
Why couldn't the pumpkin go to the Halloween party?
It had no body to go with.
What did the pumpkin say after Thanksgiving?
"Wow, I'm stuffed!"

How do you mend a broken jack-o'-lantern?
With a pumpkin patch.
What's a pumpkin's favorite genre of music?
Patch.
Why did the pumpkin cross the road?
To get to the other vine.

What do you call a pumpkin that's bad at math?

A pump-can't.

How do pumpkins travel long distances?

By gourd-plane.

What do you call a pumpkin conspiracy theorist?

A pump-king of darkness.

Why don't black cats play poker in the jungle?
Too many cheetahs.
What do you call a black cat who wins the lottery?
One lucky black cat.
Why did the black cat cross the road?
To prove to the possum it could be done.

What do you call a black cat that's stuck in a tree?
A scaredy cat.
Why don't black cats like online shopping?
They prefer cat-alogues.
What do you call a black cat magician?
Hiss-dini.

Why don't black cats play hide and seek?
Because good luck finding them.
What do you call a black cat who works at a construction site?
A fur-man.
Why was the black cat so small?
Because it only ate mice-sized portions.

What do you call a black cat who loves to bowl?
An alley cat.
Why did the black cat bring a ladder to the bar?
He heard the drinks were on the house.
What do you call a black cat who tells jokes?
A com-meow-dian.

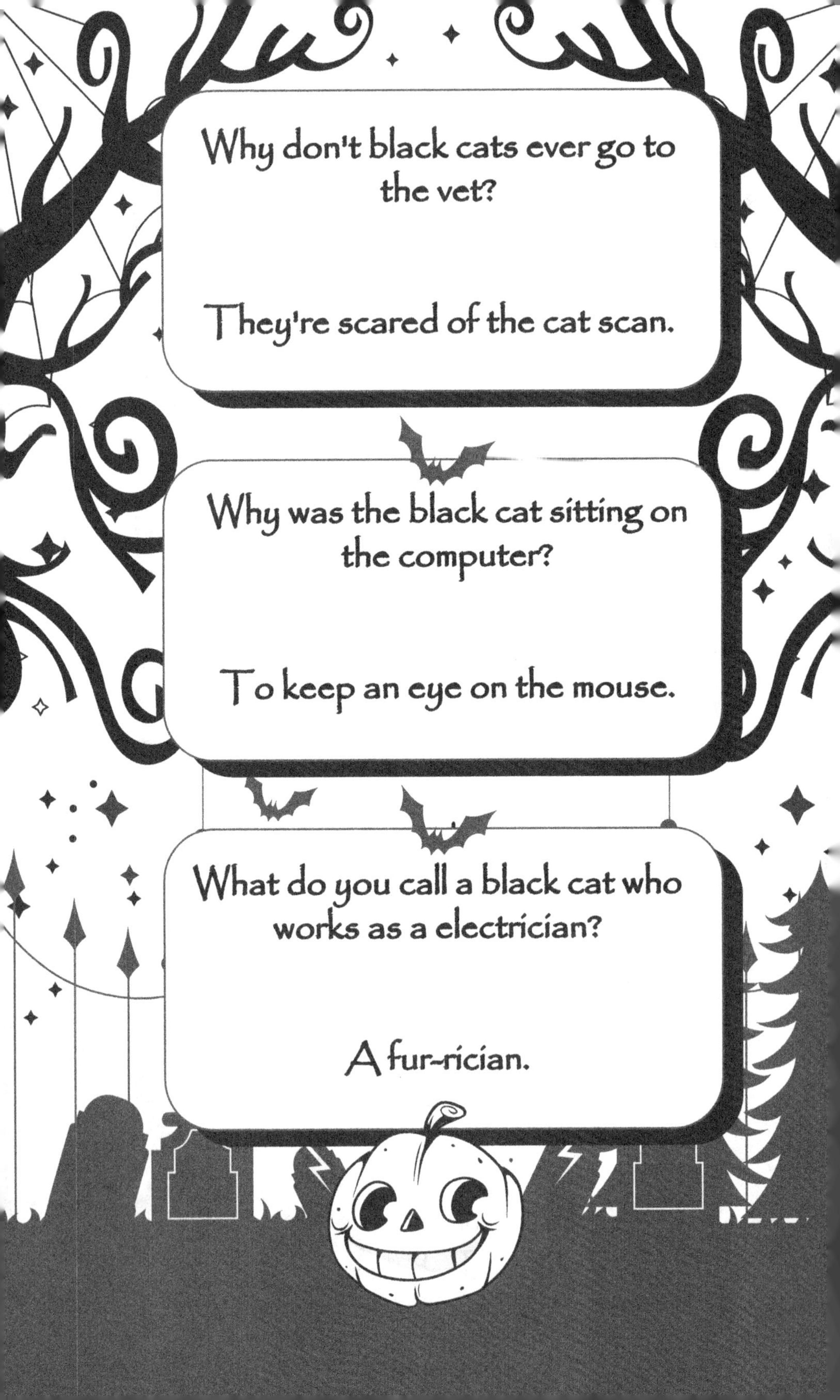
Why don't black cats ever go to the vet?
They're scared of the cat scan.
Why was the black cat sitting on the computer?
To keep an eye on the mouse.
What do you call a black cat who works as a electrician?
A fur-rician.

What do you call a bat that wins the lottery?
A lucky bat-stard.
Why don't bats like going to new places?
They prefer their old haunts.
Why are bats such good dancers?
They have great rhythm and bat-itude.

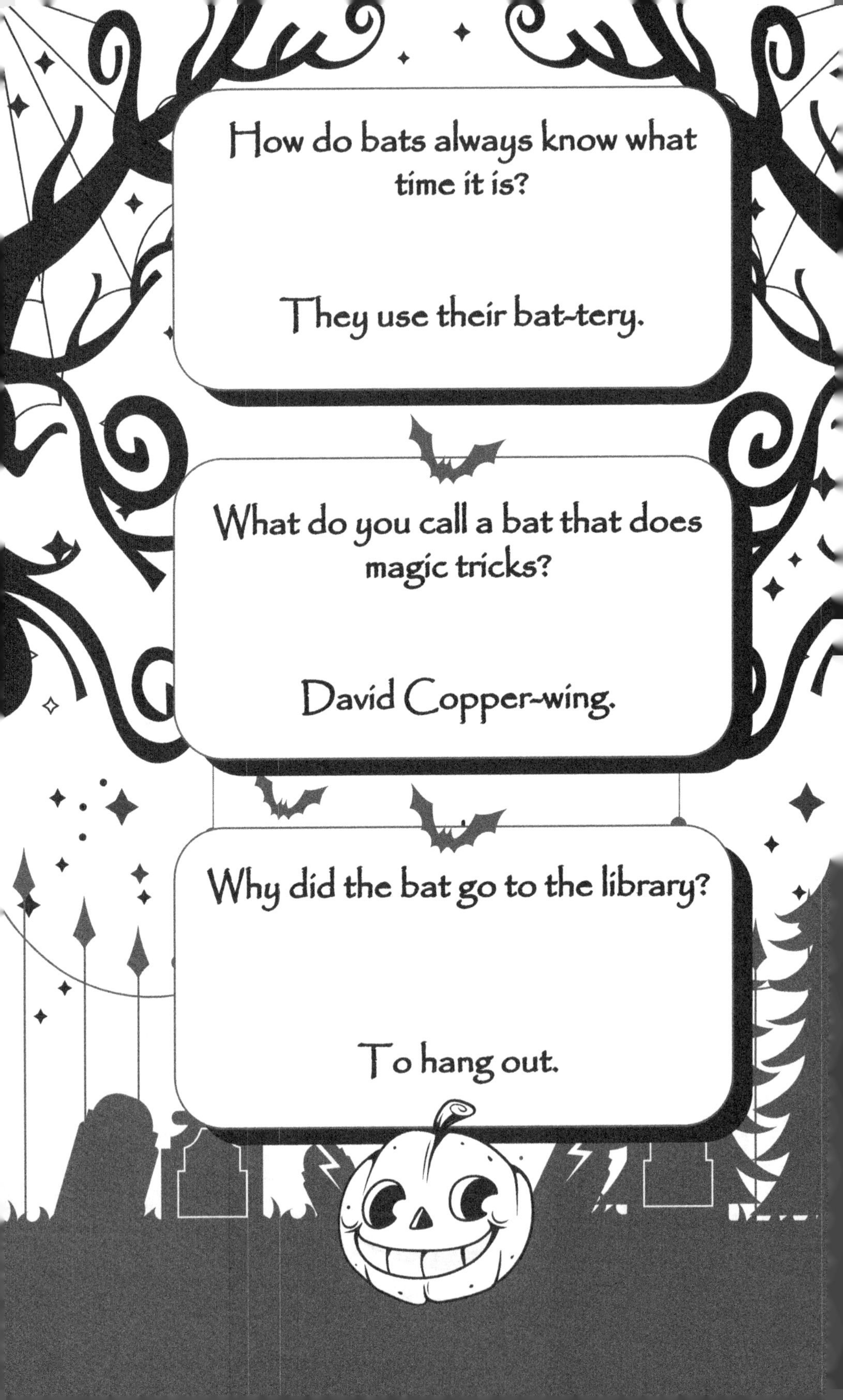
How do bats always know what time it is?
They use their bat-tery.
What do you call a bat that does magic tricks?
David Copper-wing.
Why did the bat go to the library?
To hang out.

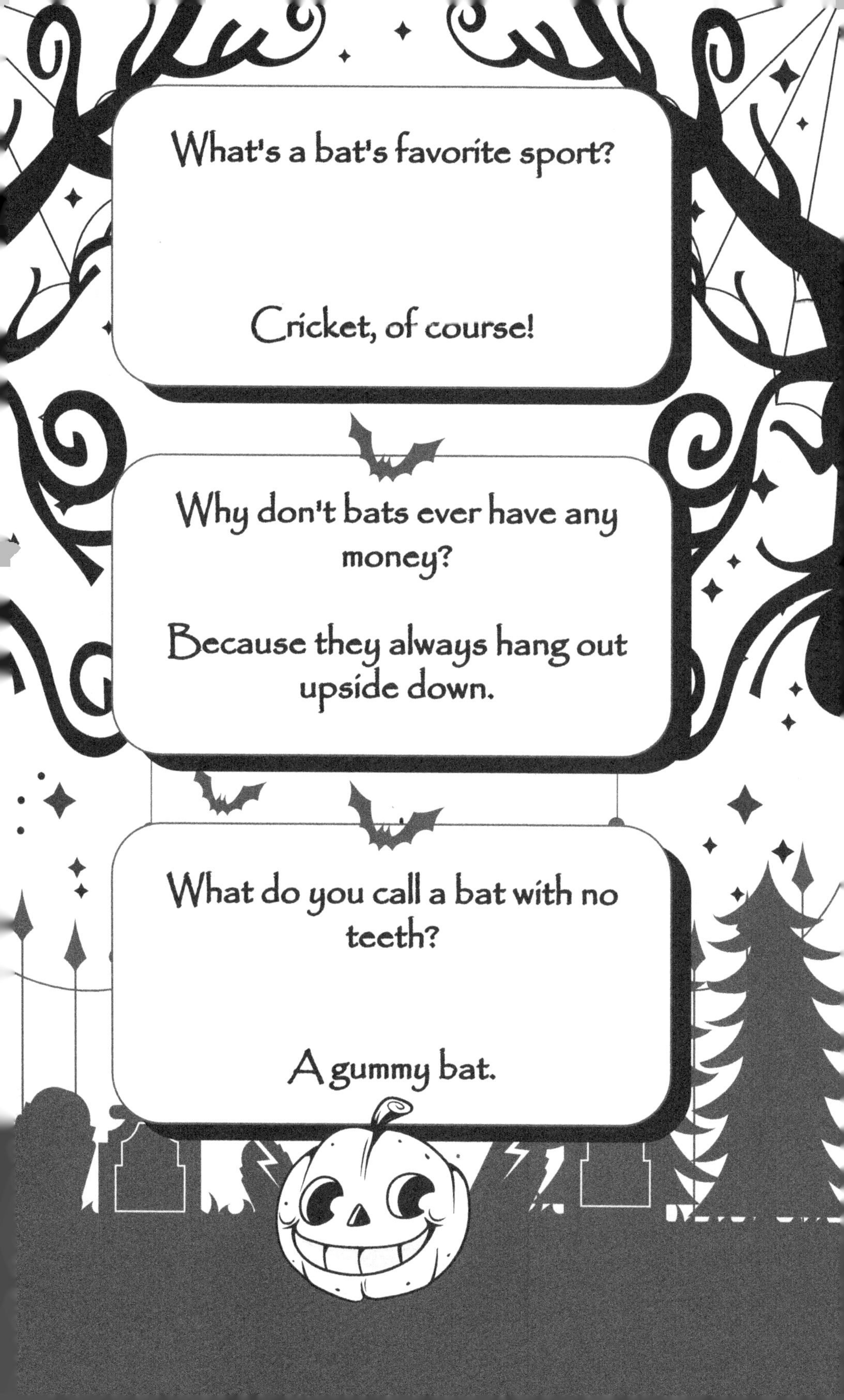

What's a bat's favorite sport?
Cricket, of course!
Why don't bats ever have any money?
Because they always hang out upside down.
What do you call a bat with no teeth?
A gummy bat.

Why did the bat take up bowling?
It wanted to improve its hang time.
What do you call a bat that's always complaining?
A whiner in the belfry.
How do bats keep in touch with their friends?
They use bat-signal.

What do you call a bat that's good at darts?
Bullseye-wing.
Why don't bats ever get married?
They prefer to hang solo.
What do you call a bat that works as a waiter?
A fruit bat.

Why are skeletons such great dancers?

They've got a lot of backbone.

What's a skeleton's favorite dance move?

The pelvis thrust.

What do you call a skeleton who won't stop dancing?

Bad to the bone.

What kind of music do dancing skeletons like best?
Rib cage.
Why did the skeleton refuse to dance at the Halloween party?
He didn't have the guts.
Why was the skeleton dancer so good at the limbo?
He was very limber.

Why are skeleton dancers always in such high spirits?
They're feeling humerus.
What do you call a skeleton's dance partner?
Their bone-amour.
Why did the skeleton win the dance competition?
He had great skull.

What's a skeleton's favorite ballet?
The Nut-cracker.
Why don't skeletons ever get tired of dancing?
They've got stamina down to the bone.
What do you call a skeleton's favorite dance?
The Monster Mash-up.

Why are spider webs so good at math?

They're great with geomet-spree.

Why did the skeleton dancer blush?

Someone called him a bone-afide star.

What dance move do skeletons do when they're excited?

They get a bone-r.

What do you call a spider web that tells jokes?
A comedy web-work.
Why don't spiders ever lose their way home?
They always take the web route.
What's a spider's favorite TV channel?
The web-flix.

Why did the spider web start a band?

It wanted to catch some sick beats.

What do you call a spider web that wins an award?

A world wide web-ner.

Why are spider webs so good at keeping secrets?

They're a tangled web of lies.

What do you call a spider web that's always gossiping?
A world wide web of rumors.
Why did the spider web go to the gym?
To work on its core.
What do you call a spider web that's good at solving crimes?
Sherlock Homes.

Why don't spider webs ever get lost?

They always stick to their plan.

What do you call a spider web that loves social media?

An Insta-gram.

Why are spider webs such good listeners?

They're always caught up in others' affairs.

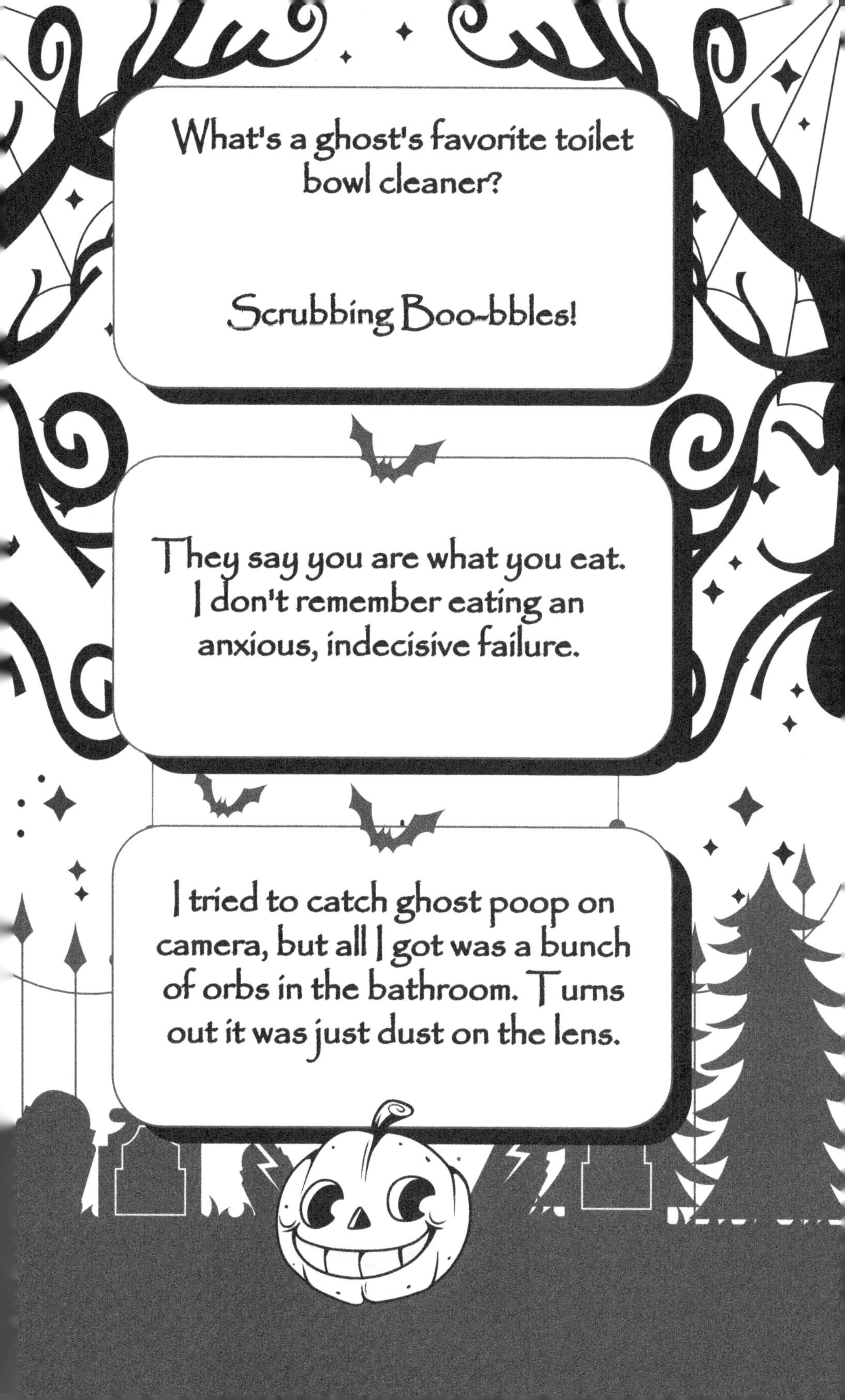
What's a ghost's favorite toilet bowl cleaner?
Scrubbing Boo-bbles!
They say you are what you eat. I don't remember eating an anxious, indecisive failure.
I tried to catch ghost poop on camera, but all I got was a bunch of orbs in the bathroom. Turns out it was just dust on the lens.

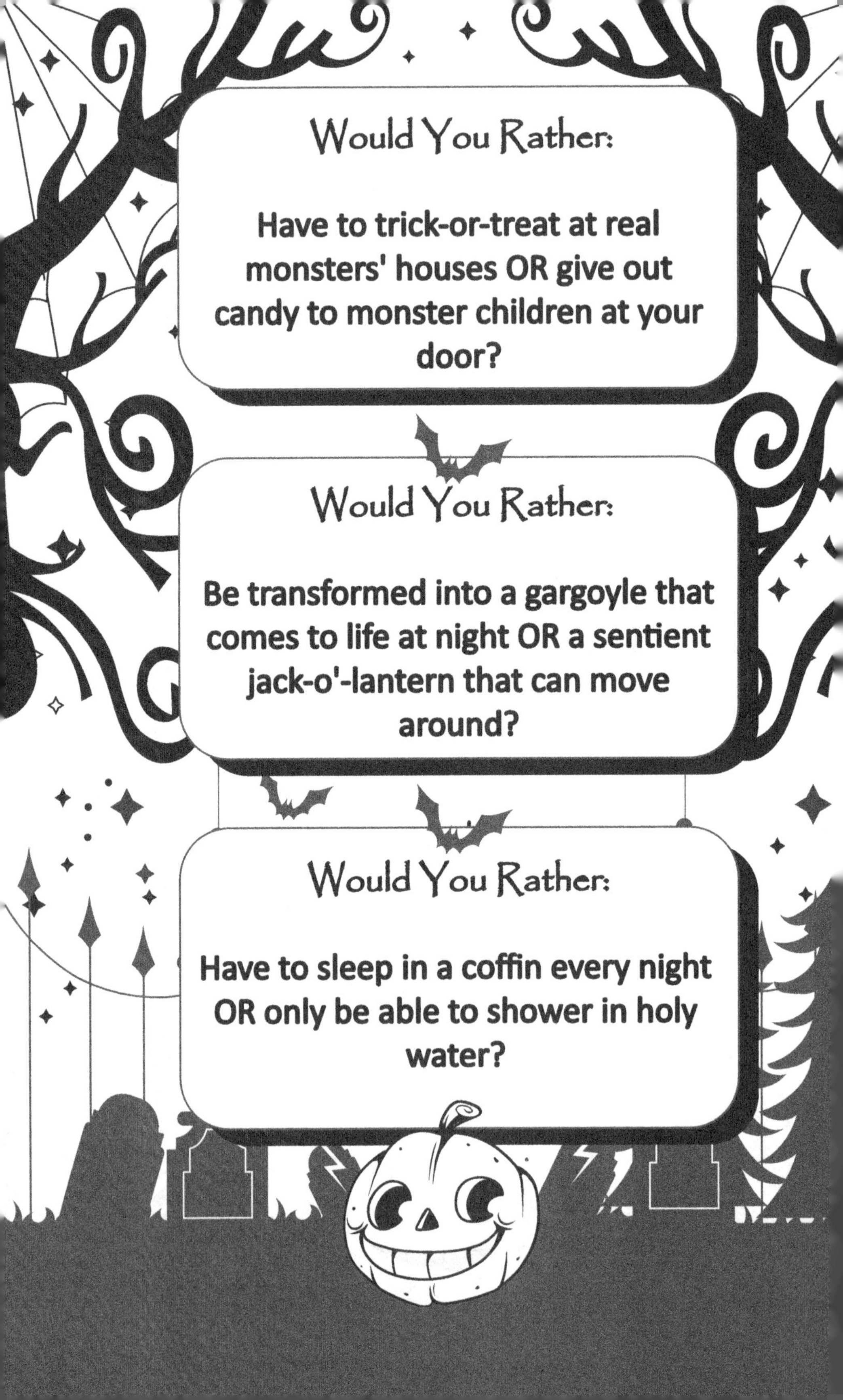

Would You Rather:

Have to trick-or-treat at real monsters' houses OR give out candy to monster children at your door?

Would You Rather:

Be transformed into a gargoyle that comes to life at night OR a sentient jack-o'-lantern that can move around?

Would You Rather:

Have to sleep in a coffin every night OR only be able to shower in holy water?

Would You Rather:

Have to live in a world where every day is Halloween but no one else realizes it OR in a world where Halloween never existed and you're the only one who remembers it?

Would You Rather:

Be cursed to turn into your Halloween costume every year but not know what it'll be OR have to wear the same horrible costume for the rest of your life?

Would You Rather:

Have to spend a night in a cemetery where all the statues come to life OR in a library where all the horror books become reality?

Made in the USA
Monee, IL
27 October 2024

68744665R00056